Blindsided

By

Marie Rochelle

Blindsided by Marie Rochelle

Red Rose™ Publishing
Publishing with a touch of Class! ™
The symbol of the Red Rose and Red Rose is a trademark of Red Rose™ Publishing

Red Rose™ Publishing

ISBN: 978-1-60435-901-5
Cover Artist: Nikita Gordyn
Editor: Cher
Line Editor: Shara Azod

Red Rose™ Publishing
www.redrosepublishing.com
Forestport, NY 13338

Prologue

Detective Lindow Woods squirmed around on the hard bench. A bead of sweat slid down the side of his face. He brushed it off with the back of his hand. His lungs felt like they were about to explode...One button on his shirt was already undone to offer some relief, but he couldn't undo another inside the crowded courtroom.

Las Vegas had been his home most of his life, so he should be used to the overly warm temperatures. But today felt unreasonably hot. He bit the inside of his mouth.

How in the hell did this happen?

Ronnie Well's didn't have two quarters to rub together, so how could he afford this high-priced attorney?

Daria Jacobs. Detective Woods was hard pressed to name an attorney who could match her. The mocha-skinned beauty moved like she owned the room while trying to get Ronnie's case dismissed on a minor driving violation.

Leaning back further on the bench, Lindow admired how the form-fitting business suit hardly suppressed her curves underneath. She had everything in the right places. He wouldn't mind asking her out on a date.

He called her a couple of days ago, trying to set up a meeting about Ronnie's case. Apparently, Ms. Daria Jacobs didn't share the same opinion about Ronnie doing time for his crimes. She hung up on him as soon as he mentioned a deal, after she'd told him in no uncertain terms where he could stick his idea.

Her fiery temper didn't scare him off. He loved a spunky woman. Sitting up straighter he forgot the uncomfortable heat as he watched Daria make her way back to the table in front of him. He wasn't about to miss the opportunity to get a better look.

By her strut, he could tell she had something to get the kid off the hook. It would be better if she could keep him from offending again.

Detective Woods hated to admit it, but he liked Ronnie Wells a lot. The kid came from a troubled home. Both parents were addicted to every drug known to man, and refused to get help from anyone. Social services granted custody of Ronnie to some rich relatives in Washington, D.C. Yet, about two years ago, out of the blue, Ronnie showed up in Las Vegas looking for his parents.

The sad thing was, after only being in town a week, he got arrested for shop lifting cigarettes, even though he wasn't a smoker. All his crimes were small until last month when an officer spotted him trying to sell drugs outside a school. After the arrest, finding no drugs on him, the station let him go for lack of evidence. However, now he was allegedly caught up in a hit and run. Ronnie looked set for jail time, until the attractive and temperamental Daria Jacobs got involved.

As she bent over the table and searched for a certain piece of paper her shirt moved, and he caught a quick glimpse of a smooth brown breast covered by a dark purple bra. It was definitely a surprise to him, making him wonder what kind of sexy underwear she liked to wear until those stuffy clothes.

God, he was glad he took a seat up front instead of in the back like he usually did. At the tempting sight, his cock became a raging hard-on in less than sixty seconds.

Maybe he shouldn't have broken up with Jackie so soon. Right now he could use some relief and no matter when he called, Jackie was always ready for a good time. He loved dating a redhead and Jackie loved dating a cop. Taking one last look at the gorgeous lawyer Ronnie Wells had defending him, Lindow got up and left the courtroom.

Attorney Daria Jacobs blew out a sigh of relief when the handsome green-eyed stranger finally moved from behind her. She felt his hawk-like eyes following her every move since she entered the courtroom with her younger cousin.

She loved Ronnie, but trouble always seemed to find him and this driving charge could get him at least six months in jail. However, she didn't think he was bad enough to be sent to jail

"Daria, how much longer is this going to take?" Ronnie grumbled pulling at his shirt sleeve.

Daria's cocoa eyes clashed with light brown ones. "Ronnie, keep quiet so I can think. God, why couldn't you just go to college like my Dad wanted?" Picking up some papers off the desk, she spun back around and gave them to the judge.

Minutes later, she strolled out of the courtroom with her younger cousin.

"I'm just not college material like you were, Cuz. This is my life," he shot back pointing, at young African American teenagers walking up and down the sidewalk.

"It doesn't have to be."

Taking him by the hand, Daria pulled Ronnie over to a bench by the courthouse doors and sat down. "Ronnie, you're a very intelligent young man. You can do anything you want to. Come on...please come back with me?" she encouraged. "I can get you set up and by next week you can be in class. Ronnie you are very lucky that I am licensed to practice law in the state of Nevada. You might not have gotten off if I left you and this case to a public defender."

Pulling his hand away, Ronnie stood up to his six foot three inch lanky frame. He stared down at her and she felt that he wanted to confide in her about something, but at twenty-one he probably thought he was too old to ask for help. She wished there was some way to make him understand he was family and family stood up for each other.

"Thanks, but no thanks," he muttered.

Bending down he kissed her on the cheek and then pushed her glasses back up her nose. "I have other plans in mind. I know how to earn money that doesn't involve spending my life in an office.

Winking at her, he turned and then ran down the steps of the blending in with the crowd.

Taking off her glasses, Daria got up from the bench and shoved them into her large black bag.

"What am I going to do about him? He can't go on living like this. It's going to get him killed," she mumbled. She was worried that the next thing Ronnie got himself into would not be easy to con his way out of.

She looked at her watch realizing she had to hurry up or she was going to miss her plane back home. Reaching down she picked up her briefcase and placed it on her shoulder. With her thoughts returning to Ronnie, she spun around, and ran into a warm, hard, and very male chest.

Two large hands reached out to steady her. "Hey, are you okay?" a deep voice asked above her.

Looking up, she stared at the man from the courtroom trying not to gasp at how unbelievable attractive he was. Moving back, Daria fixed her purse and briefcase strap back on her shoulder.

"Yes, I'm fine," she answered.

"How do you know Ronnie Wells? He's a street kid without a steady income so how could he pay for you to defend him?"

Daria stepped back away from the raw male presence he exuded.

"Who are you? Why do you care about what going on with Ronnie?"

"I'm Lindow Woods. I talked to you the other night about Ronnie needing to do some time. He's young and a few months in the slammer might just straighten him out.

That's why I've been keeping an eye on Ronnie since he came back to town. I heard how he was living with family out of state until he came back here a few months ago. Are you a relative? That's the only reason I could see why you'd be defending him."

"Why are you questioning me like I'm on the witness stand?" Daria knew this man was looking for something, but she wasn't sure what he wanted.

"I see why you became an attorney. With all that spunk you have it works perfectly for the courtroom. Are you this passionate in everything that you do?" He stared at her while he waited for her answer.

Daria shook her head in disgust while he pulled a card out of his pocket, handing it to her.

"Here you go Ms. Jacobs."

She snatched it away from him and tried not to notice how his long tanned fingers had a sexy dusting of dark hair across the back of them. She quickly scanned the card, "Yes, you're the cop that called me about helping you make Ronnie serve jail time," she snapped.

He nodded slowly. "Yes, Ms. Jacobs, I think spending a few months in jail will do Ronnie some good. Maybe help him realize jail isn't a place he wants to be at such a young age."

"Take this back. We don't need nor want any help from you," Daria shoved the card back to Detective Woods, but he wouldn't take it.

"Are you admitting that you are family?" he asked arching a brow at her. "If you are, why don't you want help from me?"

"You're going to make me miss my flight back home. Ronnie needed help and I gave it to him. Mind your business and get the hell out of my way," Daria said as she pushed past him. "Take this back, Detective Woods"

He waved a tanned hand at her. "No, you keep it you might need my help in the future."

Daria flung the card in her purse. "I seriously doubt that."

Pivoting, she raced down the steps to her car without glancing back at the smug man. She knew he was watching her from the top of the steps and she purposely made herself not look back at him.

"Oh, you never know about that Ms. Jacobs," She heard him shout at her.

Chapter One

Six months later

Pushing back the chair, Daria's gaze swung back and forth between the two men standing on the other side of the desk. Apparently Ronnie owed them and they wanted to collect. She hadn't seen Ronnie since the courthouse months ago, and even if she did know of his whereabouts, she wouldn't turn him in—not to these two.

Why in the hell would these guys think she knew were Ronnie was hiding?

"Listen, bitch we know that punk Ronnie is your cousin. So, don't even think about lying to us. We want that damn money back. We don't mind hurting you to get it, either," Marcus, the shorter one, threatened with a glint in his eye.

The taller one came around the desk and jerked her out of the seat. "See, the money he stole doesn't belong to us and the man who it does belong to wants it back."

Just the feel of his hand on her body made Daria's skin crawl. Struggling, she tried to get lose, but Gary Nolan yanked her closer to him and she felt his erection digging in her back. "I like it when a woman fights me. Keep it up and see what happens." She barely kept her lunch down as he licked the side of her neck and then roughly grabbed her breasts. He was trying to scare her, but she wasn't going to give him that satisfaction.

"Let go of my arm," Daria hissed pulling at Gary's hand. "I don't know what you're talking about."

Jamming her high heel into his foot, making him let go and she pushed past him towards the closed door. However, Marcus stepped in front easily blocking her only means of escape.

Still wincing, Gary yanked her back, wrapping his arms back around her waist to rub his cock against her again. Marcus pulled out a gun and leveled it at the middle of her chest. "I'm not like Gary. I don't want sex. I only want the fucking money. "

"Let go of me you bastard," she screamed struggling against Gary.

Daria silently prayed that someone else was still in the office. She knew that it was a slim hope because it was Friday and her co-workers left hours ago.

"Do you think we're stupid or something?" Gary growled as he jerked her arms behind her back with one of his hand. "We've been following you for weeks now. You're the only one who works late on Friday. I tried to get Marcus to let me come in by myself, but you're lucky he wouldn't let me."

"You're wrong. The security guard is here and he'll be around at any moment," she lied hoping to bide for some time.

"Nope, that John Goodman wannabe is downstairs at the front desk trying to hide his porn magazine," Marcus chuckled waving the gun at her. "Bitch, I've to give you credit for lying, though. When a woman lies it fucks with Gary's mind. I don't have a clue what he might do to you next."

Daria bit back a scream as the sound of her shirt being ripped filled the room. Gary tore open the front of her bra and grabbed her right breasts in a painful grip. "Fuck man, have you ever seen tits like this before?" Gary moaned as he pinched her nipple

Marcus shrugged his shoulder. "They're too big for me. I like tits a little smaller, but have all the fun you want. Ms. Jacobs seems to think we're playing with her about the money."

Silent tears fell down Daria's face as Gary's hand pulled up her skirt and his hand slipped beneath it. God, she didn't want him to touch her. "Let go of me, you bastard!"

"Beg me to stop and I might think about it," he hissed in her ear. "I've never been with a woman like you before. Are you as hot and tight as I think you are?" Daria felt Gary's fingers at the edge of her underwear.

She started to scream again when Marcus voice cut her off. "Gary, let her go. I don't have time for your sick games tonight."

"Come on man. I'm so close to paradise. Just give me a few minutes alone with her. Go and check on that security guard. I'll make it fast."

"Not tonight!"

Daria shivered with fear as Gary jerked her skirt back down. "I'm going to get some of you, so you better be ready," he threatened in her ear, but he didn't let go of her wrists.

Marcus looked at her with no emotion on his face. "Ronnie trusts you, so he'll contact you and don't try to keep it from us. We'll be watching you. If you don't tell us I'll let Gary come back and finish what he started. I used to think Ronnie was a bit on the dumb side, but he proved me wrong. It took a hell of a lot of balls to take that money. But, he's going to get scared and he'll get in touch with you. When he does call get in touch with us right away. We won't hurt him as long as we get that damn money back. Don't you want us out of your life?"

Marcus pulled out a piece of paper from his jeans pocket shoving it into the pocket of the ripped shirt she was wearing.

Marcus went to the door and held it open. "Let's go, Gary."

Gary let go of her arms. The relief in her arms almost made her sigh, but Daria stood statue still as Gary paused, blowing into her ear, "You can bet I'll see your sexy ass later."

Then they left, the echo of the slamming door hung in the air.

Shaking with fear, Daria collapsed on the floor staring at the closed door. Those two meant business.

What in the hell have you gotten involved in Ronnie?

Where was he?

She rubbed her wrists. Pushing herself off the carpet, Daria made her way back over to the office door and locked it and then fixed her clothes as best as she could before making it back to her chair. Her heart pounded a mile a minute, she hated to admit it but she was scared out of her mind.

Her partners at the law firm didn't even know about her defending Ronnie. The case came up during her vacation time. She didn't hesitate because she loved Ronnie like a brother. God, she didn't need this right now not when she was thinking about leaving the firm to start her own law practice.

Shutting her eyes against the bright lights in the office, Daria tried to calm down and think of a solution. If they couldn't find Ronnie, he must be missing. Perhaps she should file a missing persons report with the police department there. She closed her eyes, knowing she may have no choice but to face Lindow Woods again. He flashed in her mind taunting her to call him. Groaning, she shook her head because his arrogance made her blood boil.

Why are you lying to yourself girl? You know you found that white detective sexy the instant your eyes met his in that courtroom.

The thought of going back and asking him for help upset her to no end, but she didn't know anything about these thugs, and she needed to protect herself and her family somehow..

Opening the desk drawer, Daria pulled out Detective Woods' card which was laying on the top of several others business card she kept in there. For some reason, she could never pitch the darn thing in the trash.

Reaching for the phone she punched in his number.

Lindow heard the ringing phone beside his bed but he ignored it. There was no way in hell he was about to answer it at this time of night. Not while Jackie licked her way down his chest, he loved what she could do with that pink tongue of hers. He waited for the phone to stop, but it didn't. Snatching it up on the fifth ring, he yanked it to his ear...

"Hello," he growled.

"Is this Detective Woods?" a very soft and sexy voice asked on the other end of the phone.

Whoever who she was, she had his attention

"Yes, I am. Now tell me who you are."

"Umm...I don't know if you remember me or not but my name is Daria Jacobs. I represented Ronnie Wells about six months ago.

He remembered the sexy petite lawyer very well. She had been a fantasy in several of his day dreams until he let Jackie back in his life. Even now with her kissing his chest, his need for Jackie waned. Touching her on the shoulder, he pushed her off his body and then rolled out of the bed. Walking into the bathroom naked, he closed the door.

"Hey, who are you talking to?" Jackie yelled at him through the door. "Come back out here and talk to me!"

Lindow didn't have time to deal with Jackie's outburst, not when he had the woman he craved on the phone. "What made the rich attorney, Daria Jacobs, call a middle-class detective working narcotics at six o'clock in the evening?"

She acted so superior to him, so he couldn't resist the dig at her.

"Never mind, I can find out who these thugs looking for Ronnie are from someone else, sorry to bother you, Detective," Daria snapped disconnecting the call.

"Wait!" He yelled trying to keep her on the phone, but all he heard was a dial tone. "How in the hell...?"

He was too late. Daria didn't hear him. Lindow stared at the phone in his hands scared for the attractive attorney. If it was Gary Nolan and Marcus Mitchell she spoke of, she should be scared. Ronnie must have ripped them off. He needed to see heras soon as possible.

Rushing back into the bedroom, he was happy to see Jackie had left. He really shouldn't have let her convince him into bed. He got dressed in record time and placed a call to the station on the way to the airport. He found out Daria's current address in Washington, D.C. Sitting in the airport, Lindow wondered how Ms. Jacobs was going to react to seeing him. Hell, he knew that she wasn't coming back to Nevada without a fight.

God, he hoped Daria was ready for him because he sure was *ready* for a battle with her.

Daria stole another glance in her rearview mirror making sure that no one followed her home. She had the feeling someone was watching her since she left the office. She'd gathered up everything she had on Ronnie's cases and tied up some loose ends before leaving. Calling Woods proved a big mistake. She just knew he wouldn't help her, so she would work it out for herself. It was dark now and she prayed her unwelcome visitors wouldn't come back tonight.

She wondered if those two watched her right now, or had they been bluffing? For three hours she worked behind her locked door before she plucked up enough courage to get to her car. Normally she never left until after eleven. The long, slow drive home usually relaxed her, giving her time to think about the events of her day. However, today turned into the worst possible day of her life and she couldn't wait to get home.

Getting out of the car, Daria made a mad dash for her house because she still couldn't shake the eerie feeling someone was near. As she turned the key in the lock a hand touched her on the shoulder. She screamed and then passed out.

When Daria felt the cool cloth on her face, she opened her eyes, she saw Detective Woods leaning over her with a smirk on his handsome face. "Well, I have to say you are the first woman to ever faint at my feet," he laughed.

Shoving him back, she sat up on her couch, holding the side of her head, "What are you doing in my house?" Why in the hell did she call him? Now he was here in person to bother her sanity.

"I couldn't leave you out there on the front porch, could I? And after all, you left the key in the door, I figured it was an open invitation." He took the wet cloth from her.

"I'm safely inside my own home, so you can leave now," Daria stood up. Looking down, she noticed her shirt was open. "Why is my shirt unbuttoned?"

He raised his hands in self-defense. "I had to make sure it wasn't breathing problems causing you to faint," he answered innocently. "By the way, I like the peach bra. Very sexy," he said with a wink.

Tossing the cloth on the table, Lindow flopped down into the seat behind him. Folding his left leg over his right knee he ogled her while she fixed her clothes. She shot him a dirty look, but his eyes never strayed.

"Look, why are you here?" she snapped. "I thought I told you on the phone I didn't need your help."

Lindow got up from the couch and stood in front of her. Without her high heels she barely came to his shoulder. "Who's looking for Ronnie. Did they mention the names Gary or Marcus?"

"One was called Gary." Remembering the visit gave her a shot of panic.

"What time did they call you? Did you record the message?"

Daria looked at Detective Woods like he had a screw loose in that good looking head of his. "What phone call? They came to my office today..."

"What!" he yelled making her jump. "Did they touch you or threaten you in anyway? They must be really tired of waiting on Ronnie."

"Marcus pulled a gun on me, saying he wanted the money or else. Gary sort of made suggestive comments, but it was nothing I can't handle. I'll just give them the money and the problem will go away."

"So, did those suggestive comments you said you could handle give you these bruises?" Detective Woods held her hand up and she noticed how dark the marks were. He moved close to her, as if protecting her.

"Do you know where Ronnie is?" Daria wasn't about to confess how scared she was earlier.

He grabbed her by the arm hauling her closer to his hard body. "You're a lawyer. You should know you don't ever pay off guys like them or they will come back asking for more."

Woods continued, "We need Ronnie to testify against them. I know they are into more than just drug money. Now just tell me where he is."

Daria pulled her arm out of Detective Wood's grasp, trying hard not to notice how solid his body was against hers. God, she didn't need to be lusting after this man right now. "Like I told them, I don't know where he is. I haven't seen or heard from him since the court case." Rubbing her bare arms, she put some much needed distance between her and the too-sexy Detective.

"What else happened with them today?"

"Nothing"

"Then what is this piece of paper I pulled out of your shirt," Lindow asked, holding the sheet up between two fingers.

"Give that back to me." Daria had forgotten all about that in her concentration on how to handle this herself. She hurried over to Lindow and tried to snatch the paper back, but he held it away from her.

"Why is it so important?" He asked waving the paper above her head.

She studied the new dilemma in her life. Could she really trust him to help her? He seemed like he was interested in helping her out and finding Ronnie all at the same time. "It's a phone number they told me to call once I found out where my cousin is with their money."

"Were you going to call this number?" he questioned harshly.

"Yes," she answered, shocked by his dumb question.

"What if they gave you an address to meet them at? Would you have gone?" Lindow questioned shocked.

"Of course," Daria answered.

Lindow shoved the paper in his pocket. "I thought lawyers were intelligent. This could be a set-up to hurt you or rape you. Gary has been arrested several times for crimes against woman. You are coming back to Nevada with me until I can find a way to clear all this up."

Detective Woods was out of his mind. She wasn't going anywhere with him. She had commitments to meet. "Detective, I'm not about to go anywhere with you. I have a job and other responsibilities I have to take care of."

"Listen lady, either you come back with me willingly, or I'll carry you back kicking and screaming. Your choice," Lindow stated matter-of-factly.

Standing up to her full height Daria glared up at the attractive detective hating the way his eyes raked over her body with interest. She didn't want him paying attention to her because it would make more difficult to fight her attraction to him.

"You can't do that," she hissed.

"Yes, I can because you are a potential witness in my case," Lindow informed her.

Daria crossed her arms over her chest hating the man in front of her more by the minute. She hated that he was right. She did have to go with him to find out more about her cousin.

"Fine," she snapped. "I need to make some phone calls before I can leave with you. I've responsibilities at my job and I can't leave without telling someone."

She stalked off to her room cursing Ronnie for putting her in this position. Her real problem was going to be the man in the other room. How could she stand being around Detective Woods? The short period of time in her living room with him had her blood racing.

"Don't give too much information away," he yelled at her as she closed her bedroom door.

Lindow sauntered around the comfortable living room noticing how the space fitted Daria's take-charge attitude. There wasn't a part of the room that didn't fit her spitfire personality. All the items had a spark of interest to them. Nothing dull was in here. Even the paintings hanging on the walls had a passion about them. He wondered how someone as gorgeous as Daria Jacobs wasn't married with children. From experience, he knew lawyers worked long hours, but that didn't account for her being single.

A small smile touched the side of him mouth thinking about how she stood up to him a few minutes ago. Most men in the precinct where he worked backed down when he used that tone of voice, but not her. She stood up and faced him down as much as she could from her shorter height. At six feet six inches he was a huge man compared to the rest of his co-workers.

People took notice of him when he was out - especially women. In addition, being part Italian made him very passionate and he wouldn't mind sharing a little of his fire with Daria, who he just realized, was taking way too long in her bedroom.

"Daria, if you aren't out in the next five minutes, I'm coming in to get you," he yelled from the living room. Sitting down on her couch, he picked up a magazine off the table flipping through the pages waiting on his new assignment. They haven't even left yet and she was already causing problems.

Five minutes later Daria opened the door carrying two suitcases and a bag over her shoulder. Lindow arched an eyebrow, "Are you planning on moving in or what?"

"I need clothes to wear, don't I? I think I'll probably be held captive longer than a week, don't you, Detective?" she asked.

Standing up, Lindow moved to stand in front of Daria, "Hey if I remember correctly, you were the one who called me in panic. I was having sex when you called."

Disgust is the look he would guess crossed Daria's face as she stepped back from him. "I didn't need to know that."

Lindow ran his hand down his face. Calming his temper with several deep breaths he started over, "Okay, how about we make the best of a bad situation. I'll get back to Nevada and when I get secured, you won't have any problems with Gary and Marcus because I'll be your twenty-four hour body guard," he assured her.

"Oh, hell no! You can't be around me twenty-four seven. I'm not going. I'm perfectly fine right here."

Daria plunked down her suitcases.

He saw the dread in Daria's beautiful big brown eyes. "Don't worry, they won't get near you."

Reaching out he placed his hand on her shoulder. "I promise that I'm going to protect you."

"I don't think I want your kind of protection."

"Well, as I see it, you have no choice if you want to save that kid's butt." Lindow looked down at her and smiled as beguilingly as he could. "I promise to be a gentleman, always."

He could feel the air in the room change. She looked at him for a long time.

"Thanks," she whispered placing her hand on the top of his.

He flinched at the light touch. It made his body reacted swiftly making his cock ache with need. Oh, he had to keep his distance from her before she became a temptation he couldn't resist. He promised to behave.

Snatching his hand away, Lindow picked up her two suitcases, "Come on or we'll miss the plane," he barked.

Lindow went out the front door wondering how he was going to explain the sudden appearance of Ms. Jacobs to his boss and partner. Maybe it would have been better to deal with Marcus and Gary on his own instead of adding the alluring Daria into the mix. But he wasn't thinking straight when he smelled her alluring scent or looked at her luscious body. All he knew was that he wanted her to be near and this was the only plan he could come up with at the moment.

The second the boarded the plane Lindow started reading a magazine. Daria noticed that he never glanced in her direction once despite the fact she was sitting right next to his big warm body. Guessing this was probably the only time she would get a chance to study Detective Woods, Daria turned her head slightly and stared at the man beside her.

His thick dark brown hair looked almost black until the light picked up the brown highlight, wickedly thick brown eyebrows arched over a pair of rich green eyes. It brought her attention instantly to his long, thick, black eyelashes, something most women would kill for.

Moving down Daria noticed his strong powerful jaw line with a small scar right below his full bottom lip. Licking her lips she wondered what it would be like to kiss him and how well he could use those firm lips on her.

What?! Why am I sitting here staring at a man who hated being in the same room with me for longer than ten minutes?

She was thankful Detective Woods was totally engrossed in the magazine and didn't notice her drooling over him. Turning her head, she started out the window until sleep took a hold of her weary body.

Finally, Lindow thought. Daria's intense stare was about to make him yank her tempting body into his arms for a sample of her full, pouty lips. Shit, why did she have to search his face like that? He wasn't any different from any other man, but she seemed to think he was. He noticed it the first time he saw her back in the courtroom, for some reason her eyes had stayed on his body as much as his did on hers.

Damn, I don't need this crap.

Out of everyone at work why did he have to be the one assigned to the Ronnie Wells' case? It was like fate was out to get him. Didn't he already have enough problems without adding the gorgeous woman asleep beside him? However, he did admire her take charge attitude and sharp mind.

Lindow knew that if Marcus and Gary hadn't scared the hell out of her, Daria would have *never* called him. He had waited for over a month for a phone call from her and it never came until now. Without a doubt, she didn't like asking for help and it was killing her to take it now from him. A soft moan coming from her lips drew his attention back to his sexy traveling companion.

He noticed how she was pressed against the window, so she wouldn't touch him during her nap. He didn't know if he was upset or pleased by the fact. The outfit she changed into wasn't a bit sexy, but his mind was running wild at the possibility of being able to take it off her. The thin red strap top matched with the flowing white skirt added to richness to her tone. Lindow tried to resist the urge to touch her, yet it was a losing battle and he knew it.

Sliding the magazine back into the proper place, he ran a finger down her bare arm shocked by the silkiness of her skin. All of her jet-black hair was pulled into a tight bun at her nape with three hairpins. He knew he shouldn't, but he wanted to see her hair down easing closer to her sleeping body he slid the hairpins from her hair allowing it to fall to her shoulders.

Gently, Lindow ran his fingers through the thick glossy mass of hair. Suddenly, Daria whimpered in her sleep and he quickly dropped his hand. Lindow knew that if he touched her again it would wake her completely, so instead he closed his eyes for a light nap. Hopefully his thoughts wouldn't be filled with the woman beside him.

"Are you sure it's safe here for me?"

"Yes...it's very safe here Ms Jacobs. You don't have a thing to worry about and the guys don't even know that we are back here in Nevada. Everything should be fine and very secure for you," Lindow tried to assure her in a comforting voice.

Nodding her head, Daria wandered around the room wondering what she was suppose to do in this huge lonely room.

"We'll have different officers checking on you through the day, but I am the main person assigned to you."

Lindow eyed her for a few minutes and then said. "Is there anything you need before I go to bed for the night?

Yes...there was more, but she decided to let it down until another time. "No, I'll be fine."

"Look, I'll check in getting you some books and magazine, okay?" He sighed acting like the whole situation was getting on his nerves.

"I don't need anything I brought some paperwork to catch up on," She answered wishing this situation was already over.

Detective Woods paused in front of her like he wanted to say more, but Daria wished that he would just hurry up and leave. "I'll see you tomorrow, okay," he said softly and then headed for the door." Remember, you can't leave this room," he reminded her.

"I know I can't," she snapped.

"Good," Lindow replied. He opened the door and then closed it behind him with a loud click.

Pausing in the middle of the room, Daria got an uneasy feeling in the pit of her stomach like something wasn't quite right. Maybe she call Detective Woods back and make him stay a little longer with her. No, he had already checked all the rooms and nothing was wrong with leaving her here. Everything would be okay.

Chapter Two

For hours after Detective Woods' left Daria wandered around the bedroom before she finally decided to get some work done. She hated being caged in like this. There was only so much paper work person could do without losing her mind.

Could someone please deliver me from this evil?

After about thirty minutes of getting nothing done, she tossed the file on the table and decided to take a shower and turn in early. Maybe a good night's sleep was something she needed and just didn't know it yet. Daria picked up her robe off the bed, she carried it into the bathroom and hung it on the back of the door. Turning the shower of full blast, she pulled her hair back into a light ponytail and then stepped beneath the powerful spray.

Daria allowed the massaging feel of the water pouring down her body to relax the tension from her body and erase the events of the day. She wanted to climb into bed with an empty mind and fall straight too sleep. One thing she hated was tossing and turning in the bed for hours.

Her hand was reaching for a bottle of shampoo to wash her hair when the shower curtain was yanked back and a pair of strong hands jerked her from the shower. Pure terror raced through her body making it impossible to scream. She kicked at the intruder legs and tried to wipe the water from her eyes with the back of her fingers.

Callous hands shoved her dripping body down on the cold tile floor. Finally after getting the water out of her eyes, Daria opened her eyes and found Gary looming above her.

"OH MY GOD!" She screamed twisting her body trying to get Gary off but her struggles weren't doing any good, he was too strong.

"Bitch, didn't I say I would be back?" His sour breath hissed in her face. The fetid smell almost made her vomit in her mouth. "Damn baby I knew you would have a good body," Gary drooled as he ran his palms over her breasts, "but this is unbelievable."

Daria knew if she didn't find a way out Gary was going to rape her. While his attention was distracted with her body she looked around for a weapon. She had almost gave up hope until she spotted a paperclip laying a few inches from her fingers. Grabbing it with her fingertips, she slowly worked it open praying Gary wouldn't notice what she was doing.

Finally after getting it undone she twisted her body again trying to get him off. "Get the fuck off of me! You sick son of a bitch!"

Gary was still running his slim hands over her breasts whispering sickening words to her and started rubbing his erection between her legs. He only stopped long enough to glare at her with an obsessed look in his eyes. It sent a shiver down her spine. "Stop moving or I'll snap that pretty neck."

Nodding, Daria relaxed her body knowing her one and only chance was about to come. As Gary lowered his mouth to her breasts she shoved the paperclip all the way in his ear and shoved his screaming body off of hers. She snatched her robe off the door and ran from the room out of the door marked exit at the end of the hallway.

Once Daria made it to the street wearing only her bathrobe, she roamed around trying to remember the street and address Detective Woods told her he lived on. The sounds of music playing from clubs and customers laughing filtered from buildings outside to her through the open windows, but she didn't let that sidetrack her. She had to get to Lindow's house. She kept walking and blocked out the odd stares from people on the sidewalk that she passed on the way there. Daria sent up a pray of thanks when she finally made it to Detective Woods' house. Stepping on the porch, she banged on the front door and then slid to the ground hoping he was home and not at work.

Shaking the sleep from his head, Lindow knew he had heard knocking at his door and wondered who it was at this time of night. Pulling on a robe over his naked body, he made his way to the front door but once he got there the knocking had stopped. He was about to return to bed when something made him open the front door. Indescribable alarm rocketed through his body when his eyes landed on Daria curled up in a ball on his porch on wearing only a pink robe.

"What in the hell?!" he uttered.

Lifting her body up into his arms, he kicked the door closed his foot and carried her back into his bed He leaned over her and ran tap the side of her face with his hand. "Daria, how did you get here? Look at me. Who brought you here?"

Opening glassy eyes, she stared back at him before her screams filled his empty house. "No...don't touch me!" She shoved at his chest like a mad woman, but he knew he wasn't the person she was really seeing. What in the fuck happened to her after he left the hotel?

"Baby, don't do that," he whispered pulling her shaking body into his arms. "Tell me what happened," he whispered above her head.

Taking a deep breath, Daria laid her head on his shoulder and placed her smooth hand inside his open robe touching his bare chest. Lindow pressed his lips together and swallowed down a moan. Damn her touch was better than he could ever imagine, but he couldn't be lusting after her right now. She needed his help and he had to find out what happened to her.

"I was in the shower when Gary pulled me out and flung me down on the floor. He told me he was keeping his promise about coming back for a taste of me," she whispered shaking.

He would kill that low life street bum when he got his hands on him. He despised men that took advantage of a woman. Daria didn't know how lucky she was to escape from Gary, because he wouldn't have let her go until he was good and ready.

Lindow pulled her closer to his body. Holding still, he whispered, "Did he rape you?"

Tremors continued to shake her small frame and it tore at his heart. "No, I found a paperclip on the floor and while he was touching me I shoved it into his ear. When he fell off on me screaming I jumped up grabbed my robe and came here," she finished on a sob.

Lindow wrapped Daria tighter against his chest wanting to hold her forever. For reasons he wasn't ready to address yet, Daria brought out his protective side. "Listen, I need to call this in and then we need to go back to the hotel."

Shoving at his chest, Daria jerked back from him and got up off the bed. "Have you lost your mind? I'm not going back in that room. How could you ever suggest it? I had to fight to leave it and you actually want me to go back there."

Spinning around she rushed from the room and he was right on her heels stopping her in the living room. "Daria, wait one minute."

However, she kept moving away from him like she hadn't heard a word that came out of his mouth.

"Damn it, I said wait," he growled, grabbing her arm. "I won't make you go back there. You can stay here with me."

Large brown eyes stared back at him with apprehension, "Why are you doing this? You could stick me in another hotel."

"No, I don't think so, they aren't as safe as I first thought." He would have to talk with his captain about this. Someone told Gary what room Daria was staying in and he was going to find out who in the hell it was.

"Won't your girlfriend get upset with me being here?"

He let go of Daria's arm and ran his fingers through his hair. "Jackie isn't my girlfriend.

"Oh," Daria replied and then gave him a wary look before she put a little distance between them.

"God, don't look at me like that. You don't have to worry about me bothering you."

Daria's eyes hardened at his cruel comment. "Good, I didn't think a guy like you would be."

He advanced on Daria, jerking her back into his arms. "What is that supposed to mean?"

"Nothing Detective Woods, now can you please let go of my arms?"

Lindow pushed Daria's tempting body away from his and stormed back to his bedroom. Twenty minutes later he came back out fully dressed and found Daria standing in the same spot rubbing her arms. He instantly felt bad for the way he just treated her. None of this was her fault, but she was in it knee deep now.

"Hey, do you need me to bring someone back so you can talk to them?"

She crossed her arms under her breasts and shook her head. "No, I'm fine."

Lindow came closer to her and stopped when her body tensed up. "I don't know how long I'll be gone, but try to get some sleep in the guestroom if you can. It's right down the hall from mine. It's the first door on the left," he said touching her briefly on the shoulder and then he left.

Wrapping the robe more securely around her body, Daria decided to take Detective Woods advice. She went over to the couch and laid down. She was so tired. It wouldn't hurt if she took a little nap until Detective Woods came back home and then she would book the first flight back home.

Hours later, Lindow came back home without the answers that he wanted. No one at the department knew how Gary was able to find out about Daria's location. His boss wasn't pleased that she was staying with him, but he dropped it in the end.

He was headed back to check on Daria in the guestroom when a sound from the couch caught his attention. Glancing over his shoulder, he groaned when he spot Daria curled up there sound asleep.

He made his way over to her bending down he brushed a lock of hair away from her cheek. "I didn't want you to sleep on the couch, *Innamorata*."

Picking her up, he carried Daria to his bedroom and gently placed her in the middle of his bed.

"You can't sleep in that robe."

Walking over to his closet, he pulled out a large black T-shirt knowing it would cover her smaller frame completely.

Untying the robe, he quickly pulled the shirt over the head and tried his best not to wake her up or notice the appetizing body before him. Sliding her under the covers, he touched her cheek before leaving the room. He brought her suitcase back with him but they were in the car. He would place them in the guest room and hopefully tomorrow, she would come down to the station and give a statement.

The next morning Daria searched Lindow's house looking for the kitchen half asleep. She wasn't any good until she had her morning coffee. She finally found it after five minutes, but she got the shock of her life when went through the kitchen door.

Detective Woods was relaxing against the counter wearing tight blue jeans. A snug dark blue T-shirt with stretched across his wide chest and a steaming cup of coffee was in his hand. Green eyes watched her over the rim causing her to pull the shirt more snugly around her body.

"Where's my robe? How did I end up back in your bed?" Daria asked.

"*Buona mattina, bella*," he replied.

"What did you say?"

Tossing his unfinished coffee down the sink Lindow answered her, "I said good morning."

"Wasn't that Italian?" she asking, interested in learning more about him.

"Yeah, my mother taught me a long time ago," he answered quickly ending the conversation before it began.

She got the hint and left it alone. "So, are you going to answer my question, Detective?"

"I came home and found you asleep on the couch still wearing the wet robe. So, I knew you couldn't stay in it and I took it off and gave you one of my shirts."

Daria's mouth opened, but no words could get back her tight throat. He undressed her?

Her silence seemed to piss him off because he snapped at her. "Don't worry I didn't try anything with you. Remember I did say I would be a gentleman and I wasn't lying."

She couldn't believe the gall of him and wanted to tell him what she thought, but she kept her mouth shut and kept her nasty reply to herself. Pulling the shirt away from her body she said, "You don't think I'm going to wear your shirt all day do you?"

Lindow let his eyes roam over Daria's cute shapely body thinking how he wouldn't mind seeing her without the shirt. Daria had a deliciousness about her that was hard to ignore and one thing he enjoyed was a good-looking woman. Even if the one he wanted right now was glaring at him through narrowed eyes.

"No, I brought your clothes home from the hotel last night and they're in the guest bedroom. I'll give you time to change so you can go down to the station with me and give a statement."

"You didn't mention anything about a statement last night," Daria said moving to sit down at the kitchen table.

"Do you want Gary to get away with what he did to you?" Lindow asked moving to squat down in front of her. He touched lightly on the back of her hand. She willed her body not to respond to the touch but it was hard with his cologne surrounding her senses.

"Of course not," she exclaimed.

"Wonderful, go get changed and we can go."

"How will I get back here?" she asked rising from the table at the same time he stood up causing her breasts to brush his chest. His breath hissed from his body while she tried to move back from the contract, but the chair behind her prevented it.

Moving back, Lindow allowed her to slide by his tall body, "I'll have an officer bring you back after you're done." She stared up into his eyes then rushed from the room, but not before she heard him mumble, "You can't allow yourself to feel anything for her."

Chapter Three

Several pairs of eyes watched Detective Woods as he escorted her into the precinct with his hand in the small of her back. He took her to his desk and pointed at an empty seat. "You can sit right here while I go find my partner," he stated then walked away in the opposite direction.

She had never liked being in a police station although her job called for it many times. Daria felt the intense stares of the other officers on her body and how they studied her movements. How she didn't want to be here, but rather at home working on a new case. What if her baby cousin was already dead or involved in a horrible crime? If he had done something, illegal this time she wouldn't be able to get him out of it.

Why didn't he come back home with her to Washington, D.C. when she asked? But she knew with the stubborn streak Ronnie had in him it wouldn't have happened. He didn't like being told what to do unless it was on his own terms.

Detective Woods didn't know how lucky he talked her into coming down here this morning. She almost told him to forget it, but she didn't want Gary left out on the streets harming another innocent woman. What if she hadn't found the paperclip to shove into his ear to get away? The thought of being rape by him still sent chills down her spine.

"Ms Jacobs, I would like for you to meet my partner, Detective Anthony Jordan," Lindow said behind her interrupting her thoughts.

Spinning around in her chair, Daria found a pair of hazel eyes staring down at her with disinterest, "Nice to meet you, Detective Jordan."

"However, we all call him A. J. around here," Lindow said slapping his partner on the back.

Daria was stunned to find some like Detective Jordan working with alongside Lindow Woods. A. J. with his coffee colored skin, muscular frame showed by two buttons were undone on his shirt. His hair was cut close to his head almost making him appeared bald until you looked more closely. Detective A. J. looked more like a football player than a cop and he didn't look too pleased to see her.

"Lindow tells me you were attacked last night in your hotel room by Gary Nolan," he said sitting down at the desk in front of her.

Lindow pulled up a chair beside her and sat down

"Are you sure it was Gary Nolan, because he has been accused of other rapes and later the charges were dropped."

"I wasn't raped," Daria said looking at him.

"If you weren't rape what exactly happened then." A. J. asked with a hint of doubt in his voice.

She sat up higher in the chair not liking what he was implying. "He was trying to attack me, but I stabbed him and got away."

"Well, Ms. Jacobs you're a very lucky lady because Gary usually doesn't let anyone see his face. Why were you so different?"

"I don't know Detective Jordan, but are you implying I'm lying about my attack?" she questioned a hint of anger in her voice.

"No, we found blood in the bathroom along with the paperclip you used. I'm just surprised Gary was so careless this time," Detective Jordan answered taking a quick look at Lindow across from him.

"I think this was a bad idea," Daria complained jumping up from the chair. "I shouldn't have come here in the first place." She moved around Lindow and headed for the door as fast as her legs could carry her.

"You can't leave," Lindow yelled at her back, but she kept walking right out the front door ignoring him.

"Shit, what is your problem A. J.?" He yelled at his friend.

"How do we know she isn't a part of the scheme?" A.J. replied angrily. "We have had things like this happen before and you know we have. They'll lure you in with an attractive woman while all along they are moving in for the kill."

"Daria isn't a part of this. You didn't see how upset she was last night at my house," Lindow stressed.

"See, I can't understand why you took a total stranger into your home. It doesn't matter she's one of the best looking woman I've seen in a long time. Ms Jacobs still could be a criminal. A law degree doesn't mean she's innocent."

Lindow raised his tall frame out of the chair and towered over his partner who was still seated. "I know how to read people and I think she's innocent in all of this. Now, I have to find her."

Spinning on his heel, he strolled out the busy police station hoping he could catch up with Daria.

"You show her who's boss," a fellow officer howled after him.

Lindow kept going without responding. Pushing the door open, he went outside and was surprised to see Daria sitting on the front step. "I thought you had left," he stated sitting beside her.

"Don't worry as soon as I get back to your place I'm out of here," she informed him. "I don't put up with that crap from my brothers and I won't tolerate it from a man I barely know. How dare he accuse me of being involved in my cousin's disappearance? So, find someone else to help you with your case."

"Sorry, I can't do that," Lindow apologized. "You really need to finish your statement and look through mug shots to identify Marcus and Gary."

Moving her head she pinned him with a bold stare, "I'm not talking to your partner again. I wouldn't ask him for a glass of water if I was dying of thirst."

Lindow chuckled at Daria's quick temper. "I don't think you have anything to worry about. A. J. isn't too fond of you either, Ms. Jacobs. How about I'll take your statement and after everything is done? I'll drive you back to my house." Standing up, he held the door open and waved her back inside, "After you, sweetheart."

Daria brushed past him tense and ready for a fight. "Don't call me sweetheart."

"Okay, darling, I won't." He grinned following Daria back into the station.

It was past one o'clock when Detective Woods finally let her leave the station and it wasn't a moment too soon. A.J. purposely questioned her every comment tossing in off handed commentary when he could.

"I really dislike your partner. He's way too cocky." Daria had tried keeping her opinions to herself but she couldn't.

"He feels the same way about you," Lindow informed her as he made a left handed turn onto his street. "A.J. thinks you're a danger to yourself."

"How dare he!" Daria hissed. She hated when a man had a problem with her independence.

"Look...we're almost to my house. How about I fix you something to eat and we can leave your experience with my partner back at the station?"

"Who is that woman?" she asked, pointing towards the house instead of answering his question. She was surprised to see the tall redhead waiting for them. Was she Lindow's girlfriend? Jealousy rose quickly in her chest before she shoved it back down. Detective Woods wasn't hers and her possessive attitude was uncalled for.

Lindow cursed under his breath as he switched off the engine. Turning in his he said, "Whatever you do don't let Jackie get you into an argument. I know you've a quick temper and Jackie loves to push people to the limit."

Handing her his keys he continued, "Here I want you to unlock the door and go on inside the house."

"I don't like been told what to do," Daria grumbled.

"Can you please just not argue with me? Just go inside the house and wait for me there." Opening the driver's side door, Lindow got out and closed it behind him and then walked over to the Jackie.

"Jackie, what are you doing here?" She heard Lindow asked through the open car window as she debated if she wanted to get out or not.

"I wanted to surprise you and take you out to dinner," Jackie replied glaring at her inside the car.

Lindow looked back over his shoulder at her and then gave his attention back to Jackie. "I thought I told you I would get in touch with you"

Getting out of the car, Daria stood behind Lindow as she waited for the woman to answer his question. She could tell by the hard look on Jackie's face that she wasn't going to like the answer.

"Is this girl who you replaced me with?" she spat at Lindow. "I know you didn't dump me for that," Jackie hissed pointing a long red fingernail at Daria.

"What do you mean by that?" Daria yelled moving past Lindow's large body.

She was about to give Jackie a piece of her mind, but he quickly grabbed her by the arm halting her movements and then whispered in her ear. "Go in the house now."

"Fine!" Jerking her arm loose she shoved past Jackie and heard, "Hey, I thought black women enjoyed fighting over their men."

She wasn't about to take that from a woman she didn't know. "Listen, here I don't know who you are, but I'll make sure you remember me if you don't shut up." Daria threatened spinning away from the door.

"Get in the house now!" Lindow shouted at her as he tugged Jackie back towards her car that was parked at the side of the street.

Twisting the key in the lock she pushed open the front door. Banging it closed behind her, Daria hurried over to the window and watched and listened as Lindow dealt with his ex-girlfriend.

He better give it to her good or I will.

"I don't want to see you around here again. I told you to wait until I called and you didn't so now it's over." He shoved a struggling Jackie back into her car.

Closing the door, he waved her off and then moved back in the direction of the house. Daria ducked away from the window praying he hadn't seen her and raced for her room. She was tired of dealing with all of the drama in Lindow's life. It was past time for her to go home.

"Where are you?" Lindow asked the second the front door closed behind him. He paused for a few minutes and waited for Daria to answer him, but when she didn't he went looking for her. After dealing with Jackie he wasn't in the mood for Daria and her games. He came through the guest bedroom door at the exact time she was dragging a suitcase out of the closet. "Where in the hell do you think you're going, Ms Jacobs?"

"Back home to Washington, D.C. I don't have time to deal with this kind of abuse from the people around you," Daria responded without missing a beat. She tossed the suitcase on the bed and became filling it with clothes. "First, your partner and now your crazy girlfriend, I just don't need the hassle. I have enough going on in my life without adding your problems to it."

Moving over to Daria, Lindow removed the suitcase from the bed and placed it on the floor. "I'm sorry you can't leave until this case is solved."

Running up to him, Daria jabbed her finger in the middle his chest she said, "I can leave anytime I want to and I chose now."

He looked down at the finger touching his chest and he knew that he shouldn't do what he was thinking, but he needed to ease the stress they were both feeling. Wrapping his arm around Daria's wrist, he tugged her to him and without giving her time to think he captured her mouth with his.

White hot desire raced through his blood at the sweetness of Daria's mouth. It was so pure that he almost lost his grip on her. He had kissed a lot of women in his past, but none of them made his body tingling.

Using his tongue he made long sweeping, swirling motions inside Daria's mouth trying to draw the response he wanted from her. His mind raced with several different emotions from her taste to pleasure to gaining satisfaction. He wasn't wrong, she did taste as good as she looked.

Wanting more, he eased her closer to his throbbing cock hoping to alleviate some of the ache. Lindow was perfectly content to go on kissing her forever, unlike Daria who was fighting the deeper emotions growing between them. He wanted to work his charm on her, but she wasn't having it.

"Daria, do you know how much I want you?" He breathed against her lips. "I have dreamt about this since I first laid eyes on you in the courtroom. Baby, tell me you feel the same way."

Separating their mouths Daria shoved him away from her, "What are you doing?" She murmured pressing the tips of her fingers to her mouth.

He wiped her lipstick from his mouth liking the faint taste of watermelon that lingered there and her spark of temper was making him hotter. "I usually do what I want, and Daria I had the most uncontrollable urge to kiss your full lips. I know you enjoyed it as much as I did, sweetheart."

Placing her hands on her hips Daria glared up at him. "I didn't take pleasure from having your lips on mine and don't try it again. We have already established that we don't like each other." She finished before storming out of her bedroom.

Lindow watched Daria's departure with knowing eyes, "Keep denying it and I'll keep doiñg it until you admit how much you want," he whispered to her back. Laughing he followed his feisty houseguest back into the other room.

He noticed how tightly coiled her petite body was as she looked out the living room window and felt a little bad for rushing their first kiss. "Yeah, don't let the kiss worry you," he said with a light joking voice.

Daria turned from the window and faced him. "Stop being so into yourself," she sighed. "I wasn't thinking about you." She moved away from the window and took a seat on the couch.

A long, audible breath escaped Lindow's mouth as he tried to think of a way to approach her. Daria was going to be here more than a week and he wanted the experience to be pleasurable for both of them. For the first time in years, he might have found a woman who he was willingly to invest some time in. Daria was feisty, intelligent, and sexy as hell and a hard nut to crack. All the things he found appealing in a woman.

"Have you always been close to Ronnie?" he asked sitting down in a chair across from her.

Daria regarded him with a speculative gaze like she didn't know if it was Detective Woods or Lindow asking her the questions. "Am I being questioned about something, Detective?" She responded in her lawyer's voice.

"If I wanted to question you, Daria I would have taken you back down to the station. I was asking about you out of curiosity," he admitted honestly. "However, we can stay in this house and not say a word to each other." He stood up and snatched keys off the table.

"I'm going out and I'm going to leave to you own devices, Ms. Jacobs," Lindow remarked before the front door slammed shut behind him.

It wasn't long before Daria heard Detective Woods drive off. "I don't care if he left," she muttered to herself. He was pushing her last nerve on purpose and she couldn't let him win over her. She was used to dealing with complex people, however Lindow was beyond difficult. Truthfully, she didn't think there had been a word created yet to description her handsome roommate.

Stop thinking about him and get your mind focused on what's important.

Frowning, Daria dropped her head into her hands, "Ronnie, what have you gotten yourself into this time? I may not be able to save you from this one."

Ronnie was more like her little brother than her cousin. She had been the first one to hold him when he cried as a baby; it was so much fun having him in the house, because it meant she was no longer the baby in the family.

Having three older brothers drove her crazy until Ronnie came home with her daddy as a baby. After that, she loved having him around, because he always smelled so good and even when he cried it was exciting to have him in the house. Now, Ronnie was out on the streets hiding or maybe even dead.

Daria knew she had to find him. Going back into the bedroom she changed into a different outfit and left Lindow's house in search of her cousin. Six months ago, she had visited a certain part of town that knew him real well. That was going to be the first place she headed. The walk might be a little longer then she wanted to take, but it wasn't a problem as long as someone there helped her find Ronnie.

After all the drama was done and over and Ronnie was safe, he was going back on the first flight home with her. She was about three blocks away from her destination when she spotted one of the guys she spoke with during her cousin's trial. He was around the same age, but only taller.

Rushing over to him she said, "Excuse me, do you remember me?"

Ja'coby King spun around raking his eyes over the pest of a lawyer he remembered from a few months ago. She wouldn't leave him alone back then and now here she was again. He had wondered how long it would be before she showed up after it came out Ronnie was missing.

If she was smart, she would take her ass back to wherever she came from and not get involved with Ronnie anymore. Hell, he wasn't dumb enough to do what the fool cousin of hers had done. If that boy wasn't dead it was only a matter of time before he would be.

"Yes, I know who you are," he muttered easing away from her and then started walking in the opposite direction. It wouldn't do him any good to be seen with her either. He looked around to make sure nobody was looking at them.

Daria walked faster to keep up with him. "Please, wait I only want to ask you some questions. I'll pay you if I have to," she yelled after him.

There was no way in hell he was going to be seen taking money from her on the street. Was she trying to get his ass kicked or end up in the river with other people who didn't know how to keep their mouths shut?

Ja'coby stopped moving and waited so Daria could catch up with him. Twisting around he bent down close to her, "Listen lady because I'm only going to tell you this one time. Go back home and forget you had a cousin."Ronnie is in so much trouble and nothing you can do will help his ass. Not even with that fancy law degree of yours," he exclaimed as his eyes darted over Daria's shoulder. Ja'coby froze as he spotted something he didn't want to see. "You need to go back where ever you came from and fast." He warned before spinning around running off in the opposite direction down the street.

"Don't go," Daria yelled after Ja'coby, but it didn't matter, he was already around the corner out of sight.

Chapter Four

Wondering what scared Ja'coby Daria took a peek over her shoulder and spotted a black Sedan with tinted windows parked at the corner. She couldn't see anyone on the inside, but she had a feeling someone was staring at her. Feeling a little nervous she eased towards the crowd at her corner waiting to cross the street.

She didn't look back until she was safely across the street and when she did the car was gone.

"I wonder who that was," she said out loud.

Pulling a picture out of her coat, Daria stopped by the first group of teenagers she came up on and asked them did they know Ronnie. A majority of them brushed past her without even looking at the photograph. The ones who didn't blow her off really didn't give her any good information about Ronnie.

Daria soon realized that she wasn't going to get anything out of them, so she left and went another three blocks landing her into a rougher part of town. Instantly she noticed how several of the guys' eyes landed on her with an interest she didn't want.

Just as she turned to leave she heard, "Hello sexy. You didn't have to come looking for us," a familiar voice yelled at her.

Daria didn't have to look back. She knew Gary's sick voice because it still haunted her sometimes in her dreams. Taking off in a dead run her heart jumped into her throat at the sound of shoes pounding on the pavement behind her.

"Someone please help me!" She screamed as she ran past people who were just standing there looking at her. "Please call the police!"

She couldn't believe that Gary and Marcus were pursuing her and not caring who saw them chasing her down the street in the middle of the day.

"Lindow, we just got a call in. It's about the Wells' case and I think it might be of interest to you," one of his fellow officers hollered at him from across the room.

Placing his coffee cup down on his crowded desk, Lindow ran his hands across the back of his neck. The leads on Ronnie Wells' disappearance were getting cold. Any new phone calls with information would help a lot.

"What is it?" he screamed back.

Lindow knew he sounded curt, but his mind was also still on Daria and how he stormed out of the house leaving her all alone. Surely, she wouldn't do anything dumb.

"We just got three separate cell phone calls about Gary and Marcus chasing a twenty-something year old petite, African American woman. She was screaming for help as she ran down Seventh and Webster Avenue Doesn't that sound like your house guest?" The officer asked as he headed towards the break room for fresh coffee.

Panic was rioting within Lindow as he raced from the station to his car. "What in the hell is Daria doing way down there without a car?" He cursed turning on the siren. Pulling out of the parking lot, he sped in the direction the calls came from praying he wouldn't be too late.

If they got their hands on her, Daria's body wouldn't be found after Gary was finished with her. Marcus would shoot her and dump the body. Dread set in as he rounded the corner of Seventh and Webster but he didn't see Daria or her chasers anywhere in sight.

Parking the car, Lindow jumped out and listened after a few minutes he heard screams coming from the alley to his left. Pulling out his gun he called for A. J. on his radio and ran into the alley. At the very back Daria was backed into a corner with a can of mace. Gary and Marcus were in front of her trying to get it out of her hands.

"Move away from her," he barked pointing the gun at them.

Gary and Marcus swung around shocked to see him behind them, "How did you know your little house pet was here?" Gary snickered blocking Daria's path while making another grab for her.

"Man, I'm out of here. This bitch isn't worth getting sprayed by mace or shot over." Marcus exclaimed and then looked at him before taking off in the opposite end of the long alley. Lindow wasn't about to chase after Marcus and leave Daria alone with Gary. He was the bigger threat of the two.

"Why don't you step away from her and place you heads over you head. I have already called backup and they'll be here in a few minutes."

"No. I don't think I want to do that. Ms. Jacobs is one fine ass woman and I still want a piece of her, because I have to pay that bitch back for stabbing me in the ear," Gary growled.

Lindow wanted to shoot Marcus, but he couldn't risk Daria getting hurt or giving Gary the opportunity he needed to hurt her. He wasn't surprised that Marcus turned tail and ran he wasn't the stronger of the two when it came to the messy parts.

Gary was hands down the meaner of the two and he wouldn't want to leave without taking a piece of Daria's spunk with him. "Why don't you follow your friend's lead and run before I shoot you?"

Looking around Gary he made eye contact with Daria "Are you okay, sweetheart?"

Daria nodded and whispered. "Yes, I'm fine. I just want to get out of here."

He refocused his attention on the man hindering him from getting to Daria. He had to find a way to make Gary move out of the way. "I've called for backup and they're on their way." Lindow told Gary again. "Don't you hear the sirens in the distance? It's best you leave before they get here. I'm not warning you again to move away from Ms. Jacobs."

Gary glanced at him and then back at Daria like he was weighing his options and then he made a decision. "I'm not through with you," Gary screamed pointing at him. Or you either Daria." He threatened before taking off in the same direction as Marcus.

Lindow slipped his gun back into his holster then went over to Daria, who was still holding onto the can of mace for dear life. "Honey, give me the can," he coached, easing it from her stiff fingers.

He was so angry with her that he shook her. "What in the hell are you doing out here on the streets by yourself? Didn't I leave you at home?"

Twisting in his tight grip Daria finally got loose from him, but he could still see the fear lurking in her eyes from her experience with Gary and Marcus. "You weren't any in hurry to find my cousin, so I was asking around," she snapped shoving at his chest, so he would move back. She grabbed the can of mace back from him and slipped it back into her pocket.

"Are you saying I don't know how to do my job?" Lindow asked his green eyes growing darker by the second.

"If the badge fits," Daria replied looking him up and down.

"Don't test me, Daria," Lindow warned his voice deepening.

"I didn't say anything about testing you, Detective Woods," she snapped at him. "But I can go out looking for my cousin anytime I want to. I'm not going to let Gary and his sidekick scare me," she said putting on a brave face.

Lindow was too upset to see how truly scared Daria was by the experience. "When I leave you at home you better stay there," he warned taking a step closer.

"And if I don't," she asked leaving the question open.

"Don't tell me it's you two I hear screaming at each other from my car," A. J. asked rushing into the alley interrupting their conversation.

Daria didn't bother to answering his partner. She already knew A.J. didn't like her and Lindow knew the feeling was mutual. He watched as another officer came behind A.J. into the alley. He looked just as shocked to him fighting with Daria.

"I don't have to take a lecture from you, Detective," she said brushing past A. J. going back to the sidewalk.

"Where in the hell do you think you're going?" Lindow hollered.

"Your house," she screeched back at him.

Lindow cursed under his breath at her stubbornness. "Officer Davidson, please take Ms. Jacobs back to my house."

"Yes, sir," the younger officer replied hurrying to catch up with Daria.

"Once you get home don't think about leaving again," Lindow called out to her.

Daria stopped in mid-step. "What if I do?"

"Then don't except me to come and help you again, I'll let Gary and Marcus have you." Lindow threatened but he knew deep down he wouldn't. But he had to put the fear in Daria, so she wouldn't get it in her head to go out again on her own.

"Fine, I'll stay put." She snapped back and then started back towards the front of the building.

Lindow moved over a couple of steps so he could watch Daria with Officer Davidson. He didn't want her giving the rookie any trouble. With the mood she was in there was no telling what she would do. Daria got into the car and left without a problem, but he knew this was far from over.

"I know you were just scaring her, but does she know that?" A. J. asked Lindow who was still looking at the spot Daria just vacated.

"Hell, I don't know and I don't care," Lindow muttered trying to sound tougher than he felt. God, if he had been two minutes later Gary might have been all over her.

"Daria is tougher than I first thought," his partner laughed. "She has to be to come done here without any help. Did she tell you why she was out here?"

Walking around the deserted alley Lindow got a good look and remembered why he hated this part of town. The bad elements that hung on the streets would shoot you first and then rob you while you bleeding to death on the ground. A woman as petite and sheltered as Daria Jacobs wouldn't stand a chance of defending herself.

Lindow shoved his hands into his slacks displaying the muscle under his white shirt, "Daria told me she was looking for information about her cousin."

A.J. whistled and shook his head. "Damn. She's something else."

"What do you mean by that?"

"Do you know that the women who grew up here wouldn't come down this street?" However, Ms. Washington D.C. lawyer came here as if she owned it. Did she truly understand the trouble she could have gotten herself in to?"

"No. I'm pretty sure she doesn't know how lucky she was," Lindow replied, softly.

Officer Davidson told her to stay outside while he checked out Detective Wood's house. After he was finished Officer Davidson came back outside and got her. "Do I need to stay with you until Detective Woods comes home?"

"No, I'm fine here by myself," Daria answered.

Officer Davidson eyed her for a minute or two. "Will you stay here and not go back out looking for your cousin? I'll get in a lot of trouble if you lie to me and run off again."

She wasn't up to another run in with Marcus or Gary. "I promise I'm going to stay here."

"Okay, I'm going to trust you," Officer Davidson stated. "Don't make me eat my words." He turned and left out the door closing it softly behind him.

"Uh...I'm not lying. I can find something else to do to pass away the time," Daria replied.

Going into her bedroom, Daria picked up her legal pad by the nightstand took a seat at the table in the room and wrote everything down that happened today. Hoping something would stand out leading her to find where Ronnie may be. The black Sedan was a huge clue for her, because Ja'coby King had been terrified of the person in the car. Maybe they had clues to Ronnie's whereabouts.

The next time she went out hopefully the car would be there and she could get the license plate number. Gary and Marcus wouldn't keep her from finding her cousin. She didn't come all the way here from home to stay locked up in Detective Woods' house. Looking for information was part of her job and she was damn good at what she did.

A cocky detective wasn't going to stop her. How dare he say those words to her this afternoon? She didn't need or want his help. Lindow and his partner weren't moving fast enough for her. With all the time they were wasting could be costing Ronnie his life. He needed to be found as soon as possible by someone who cared about him.

To them, he was just another black male on the street causing trouble, but they didn't know about his sense of humor or how much he loved his family although he didn't show it. She made a promise to herself that Ronnie would be found alive and she was determined to keep it.

Lindow finally dragged his tired body out of the station around five o'clock that night. He made a quick stop at the grocery store and picked something up for dinner tonight. Usually on Friday night, he spent it with Jackie, but since he dumped her, he would be at home with his too sexy houseguest. Who now was probably planning a means of escape from his life? He loved the way her chest heaved when she wanted to fight with him. Back in the alley, she looked ready to take him on totally blocking out there was an audience standing there watching them.

Daria Jacobs was a tempting package, but he couldn't get involved with a woman who was part of his case. Now when the case was over it might be a different matter. A.J. kept telling him to send her back home because they didn't need her. He wasn't so sure being at home was the safest place for her. Besides he had other plans for her that Daria didn't know about.

Gary and Marcus had already paid her a visit once, what would stop them from doing it again? Daria came across like this tough, rough and "I don't need your help" female, but he could see the vulnerability in her today. She was terrified when they had her trapped in the back alley.

A. J. thought that Daria had to know more about her cousin's disappearance than she was telling him. A. J. wanted him to see if he could get something out of her since she was staying with him. However, he thought using her seemed a bit unfair, what if she truly was an innocent party in all of this?

After getting out of the car, Lindow unlocked the door and then locked it behind him. Pausing by the wall he set the security alarm and next he stopped by the kitchen. He dropped off the bags after he was finished with in search of his moody houseguest.

Lindow looked around for about for about a good ten minutes, but Daria was nowhere in sight. Where in the hell could she be? As he made his way back to the living room, he noticed the side door open. Daria wouldn't be dumb enough to be outside late at night. Fuck, he told her to stay in the house.

Flinging the door wide open, he stormed out on the porch. "What the hell are you doing outside? Didn't I tell you to stay in the house until I got home?"

Chapter Five

"I'm not a child so don't talk to me like I am," Daria muttered without looking at him. "I wanted to come outside so I did. Why does it matter to you anyway?"

"You're under my protection until this case is solved. I don't want your dead body on my hands," Lindow commented, pissed that Daria wasn't bothering to look in his direction and how her indifference made him only want her even more. Why did he have to be so attracted to her? She made him want to shake her, yell at her, and sample those full lips of hers all in the same breath.

"Oh, so you no longer want to toss me back to Gary and Marcus? I thought you didn't feel the need to protect me anymore." She flung back.

Why in the hell did he say that? Now, she wouldn't ever let him forget it. "Haven't you ever said anything during the heat of passion that you regretted later?" he questioned taking a seat beside Daria on the porch.

Daria eyed how close he was to her, but she didn't move away. He smiled at her determination not to let it show how much he bothered her. He wondered what he really had to do to break her free of the dull lawyer mask she stayed hidden behind.

"Detective Woods there isn't anything passionate between us. Furthermore, no I haven't said anything to you that I wished I could have taken back," Daria muttered giving him a hard look.

"Fine, I'll let that one slide for now."

"Good," Daria sighed from the corner of her mouth.

"How about sexual thoughts or fantasies?" He continued wanting to get a rise out of her. "Have you envisioned me naked yet?"

Daria's head swung around so fast he thought she might have snapped it. Her eyes raked over his body before she made eye contact with him. "How dare you ask me something like that!" She sputtered. "I'm here to find Ronnie, not play the lead role in your sexual..."

"Dreams?" He cut in with a cute little smirk displaying a dimple in his left cheek.

"Nightmare is more like it," Daria mumbled jumping up off the porch away from him. She tried to hurry past him back in the house, but he wasn't going to let her get one over on him. Sticking out his hand, he wrapped it around her wrist and pulled her between his legs, but Daria stumbled and landed hard against his chest.

The sudden impact caused them to fall backwards on the porch with her soft body pressed on top of his. He quickly wrapped his arms around her so she couldn't move. He liked the feel of her on top of him.

"If you wanted to be in my arms all you had to do was ask." He teased by her ear. God, what was that perfume she wearing? The light scent was turning him on like crazy. It almost made him forget that he was here to guard her. Just how much more of this verbal foreplay could he take? Daria may not want to say the words, but she felt the chemistry between them. It still burned hot like it did the first time they met six months ago outside that courthouse.

Daria started to squirm in his light hold. "Let go of me right this instant."

"I don't think so," he muttered with a shake of his head. "I like how good this feels."

"Well, I don't like how it feels and I don't like you either," Daria uttered shoving at his chest.

"That's okay because I know we both want the same thing in the end," he whispered by the side of neck drawing her wonderful scent into his body.

"What is that?" Daria asked as her small hands stopped hitting him.

"One night of unforgettable sex," he muttered before capturing her mouth with his.

Lindow ran his hands over the silk shirt covering Daria. He wondered did her bare skin feel as good as the shirt. Daria laid perfectly still on top of his as his hands moved further down to trace the curve of her butt.

Spreading his legs wider he pressed her fully against him. He wanted her to experience the effect her constant arguing had on his body. "Are you still going to deny that you don't want me too?" He taunted as her nipples hardened against his shirt.

Leaning in close to his ear, she ran the tip of her tongue over the bottom of the lobe drawing it into her mouth for a quick nibble. His erection jerked once and grew harder between them. The pain was pleasurable yet intense at the same time. God!. How he wanted to get to know this bundle of spunk better if she let him just a little bit of encouragement.

"My body may not have any sense when it comes to you, but my opinion of you hasn't changed. I wouldn't sleep with you if my life depended on it." Daria snapped shoving at him again.

Finally getting out of his grip she jumped up and glared down at him. "Keep your hands off me and we should get along fine for the rest of the time that I'm here." She warned him before rushing up the stairs back into the house.

Smirking, Lindow folded his hands behind his head and stared up at the dark sky with a handful of stars mixed in. "Daria, you better get ready to eat those words. There's too much chemistry between us not to end up tangled in the sheets on my bed." He didn't mind the chase she was giving him. It felt good to do the chasing this time especially when the woman was as gorgeous as the spitfire in his house.

Now, he just had to make sure she didn't go out and do anymore investigating on her own for her baby cousin and get her pretty little ass killed. He was still a little pissed that she confronted Marcus and Gary in the toughest part of town. He knew some seasoned veterans that wouldn't mess with that part of town.

Daria was an added problem that he didn't factor into the Ronnie Wells' case. How could he focus on finding him when all he thought about now was how to get her into his bed? He loved how she bickered with him. It was such a turn on. He was so tired of women succumbing to him all the time.

However, Ronnie needed to be found and soon, because if Marcus and his sidekick went out there hunting again, Daria might get her cousin back in pieces.

The station had been keeping tabs on the two of them since the confrontation with Daria in the alley. However, Marcus and Gary were good because even his snitches didn't know were they were hiding. He was running out of ideas and A.J. wasn't being helpful by up with any new ones.

For some reason his partner disliked Daria and he didn't have the extra energy to waste on one of A.J.'s mood swings. Pushing is body off the porch, Lindow stood and adjusted his holster. It was time for him to go back inside and check on Daria. Nothing good ever happened when he left her by herself for a long period of time. Turning, he went up the steps and back into his house.

Daria punched the four numbers into the cell phone to check her messages on her phone back home. Moving around the living room, she listened to Alison, her boss, request that she come back to work a week early. Rolling her eyes, she pressed the star symbol on the phone to delete all of her messages. She turned off the phone and tossed it back in her purse sitting on the couch. Of course, Alison wanted her to come back sooner, so she could do all his work plus hers. Did he think that she didn't know he stole credit for the last case she worked on?

Alison's best trait was taking credit for something he didn't do with the senior partners. Didn't they care she had been there almost five years compared to his two? No, they only wanted to keep it a male dominated company. She should be the one they were looking at for the partnership. Not some guy with the scent of breast milk still on his breath.

Damn it, she was almost thirty years old and had worked too many hours on cases the other lawyers tossed away not to get that promotion. Her law associates weren't the caring and giving men that they showed the public. Each and every one of them fought over the best cases, and then tossed the meaningless ones in her direction. Did Alison really think she didn't realize what a deceitful person he was?

The only other man who rubbed her the wrong way was Lindow. He was so hot, her mouth ran dry every time he walked into the room. She didn't want that to happen to her. Keeping a cool indifference between the two of them would work out for the best. He wasn't the first police officer to come on to her and she would treat him just like the rest only as a work associate.

She wasn't here to get involved with the man. She just had to forget how his kissed made her insides melt. Or how the faint scent of his cologne made her body want to lean in for a better smell. Hell, she couldn't let him know he was right that she did want a night of unbelievable sex with him.

"What am I going to do about Lindow?" She muttered frowning off into the distance.

"If you're making a list, I'll be more than happy to offer you a few suggestions." A rich voice exclaimed behind her.

Twirling around, Daria stared at Lindow relaxed in the doorway with his shoulder against the frame looking almost too good for words and she hated him and her undeniable attraction to him.

"Are you spying on me?" Daria questioned Lindow She still felt the imprint of his mouth for hers from the kiss that they shared outside.

Moving away from the doorframe, he slowly came to her across the room. He reminded her of a jungle cat with the way he sauntered with such confidence. He knew he was a good-looking man and didn't have any problems basking in it.

"No, I wasn't spying on you. I was coming to see did you want anything to eat before I went back to the station. I'm going to have someone come and stay with you for a few hours while I'm gone."

Daria quickly swallowed down her disappointment that he wouldn't be spending any more time with her tonight. She enjoyed his quick comebacks even if she wasn't ready to admit it to him yet.

"You've been spending a lot of time at work. Do you usually spend this much time away from home?"

Lindow stopped directly in front of her and once again she caught the whiff of his cologne. An aroma that could be only associated with him: mysterious and sex combined.

She had a hard time deciding which thing she liked about him the best. Was it his walk, his scent or his voice? Or was it the combination of all three that made her want to flirt with this man like they were the last two people on this earth?

"I need to solve this case about your cousin Ronnie and I don't mind working the extra hours. This situation needs all the man power it can get to find Marcus and Gary. Those two might hold the key into locating Ronnie and the missing money."

"Why would you say that? When they came to see me both of them acted like they didn't have a clue about the whereabouts of the money."

"That may or may not be true. I had a chance to arrest them in the alley, but I wasn't going to change one of them hurting you. At that moment you were more important," Lindow replied his green eyes staring down into hers.

Turning away from Detective Woods she went over to the couch and grabbed her purse. "Wonderful, I'm going with you." She couldn't just sit inside this house and do nothing in the search for Ronnie. She hadn't moved two inches before strong fingers wrapped around her upper arm.

"Now, my little spitfire where do you think you are going?" Lindow's deep voice asked above her head.

She glanced down at tan fingers circling her arm enjoying how the calloused tips felt against her skin. Drawing her eyes slowly up his wide chest, strong chin and amazing jaw line, Daria finally made contact with Lindow's eyes.

"Back to the station with you to help find Ronnie," Daria answered making the tension in the room even thicker. She wasn't about to let him tell her no she couldn't. "I'm not going to stay here while you do all the work looking for my cousin."

Chapter Six

"No, I don't think so." Lindow muttered shaking his dark head. "You're going to set the alarm and stay put with the officer I have coming over until I come back." He told her in a firm voice. "I don't need you distracting the officers at the station."

Daria couldn't believe what she was hearing. Ronnie was her flesh and blood, but Lindow didn't think she had the right to be at the station only because of the other officers couldn't keep their hormones under control?

"I can't imagine anyone at your job caring that I'm there with you. I did get attacked by Marcus and Gary three times already when you weren't around me." She informed him. "Do you want the fourth time to be the time that they succeed in getting what they want?" She asked peeling his fingers off her arm

Instead of answering her question, Lindow moved away from her and started checking the window at the front wall. "I thought you might come up with that excuse so that's why I called someone over here to watch you until I get back later on tonight." He stated tossing her a quick look.

Oh, that was the final straw, she thought stalking toward the hunk closing the curtains at the front window. He had to stop treating her like a first grader. She was a highly educated woman that dealt with criminals' everyday in her profession. She might spot something that he wouldn't see.

"How many times do I have to tell you that I don't want to be kept out of the loop about my cousin?" She uttered. "I've more right to any information that you may find than you do. I'm Ronnie's lawyer and family."

Standing behind Lindow's massive back, she poked him in it with her index finger trying to ignore how hard it was. Was it really possible for a man to be this hard all over his body?

Taking a quick glance down she noticed how well the blue jeans displayed his butt. How did he stay in this kind of shape sitting behind a desk all day? Before she could move Lindow spun around and pulled her to his chest shocking her because weren't they just having an argument?

"By working out at least two hours after work if I get the chance and some of it I get from my father." He breathed by her ear planting a kiss below her earring.

"What?" She whispered dazed by the feel of Lindow's tongue running along the side of her neck. Why wasn't she pushing him away? She never let him keep her body pressed against his for this long.

"I answered the question you mumbled under your breath," Lindow stated in a low voice. "You wanted to know how I got a body like this and I told you."

"You weren't supposed to hear that," Daria muttered trying to regain some of her common sense. She tilted her head away from his wandering mouth before he kissed her. She couldn't handle one of his toe curling kisses right now. She had to make him realize that she needed to come with him to the police station and not stay here locked away in his house.

"Don't be ashamed that you wanted to know something about me," Lindow said separating their bodies, but not before he planted a quick kiss at the side of her mouth. "There's a lot of things that I want to know about you too, my little spitfire."

"There is?" Daria asked. Taking a step back from the heat that radiated from Lindow's body, she slid her hands into the back pockets of her jeans stretching the silk shirt across her chest.

Lindow's eyes dropped down to her breasts then jerked his eyes back up to hers. The heated look he gave her body made her blood pressure kick up another notch. She tried to shake it off, but the need racing through her body wasn't going anywhere. She had to get herself under control or she might allow his kisses to finally carry her into that forbidden territory.

"Do you really want to know?" His rich voice questioned as his fingers reached out and ran over her silk covered arm. Even through the shirt she still could feel the heat from his touch and wanted more. "If you do I'll give you an honest answer."

Daria felt her willpower weakening towards the man standing in front of her. What was Lindow doing to her that she wanted to toss her golden rule out the window? She only had two golden rules in her life. One was never date any of the lawyers at her firm and the second was to never date anyone in law enforcement.

Did she want to forget how he wanted to lock up Ronnie for six months to teach him a lesson? He hadn't shown her that he was even on her cousin's side. All they kept talking about was finding the money and how Ronnie was the missing link to do that.

So why shouldn't she think that he was only flirting with her as a means to an end? He could be thinking that if he buttered her up enough that she might give him some information that she didn't have.

No, she wasn't going to let the towering perfection of a man in front of her trick her into believing he was attracted to her. He only wanted to see if she was lying about the whereabouts of her cousin.

Daria brushed Lindow's fingers off her arm and tried not to notice the frown he tossed in her direction. "I think it would be best if we kept this conversation away from any personal wants or needs."

"Oh...I think it's a little too late for that." Lindow chuckled at her. "Since I know that you like my body now, I'm going to do my best to make you want it more and more."

"No...I don't think that would be a good idea, Detective." Daria muttered with a shake of her head. How could she possible want him anymore than she already did?

"Yes...it's already the second item on my Daria to-do list," he confessed grinning at her taking a step back.

Second item, she thought staring up into a pair of eyes that grew even darker when Lindow looked at her. "Do I dare ask what's number one of that list?" Daria asked before she could stop herself. Damn, when was she going to learn to keep her big mouth shut?

Moving into her personal space again Lindow bent down until they were eye to eye, she wanted to take a step back but she didn't. He was just too damn sexy! Why did he have to be a cop? She wouldn't break her rule for him no matter how well his shoulders filled out that t-shirt.

"The number one thing is to have you stop calling me Detective Woods and have you say my name," he muttered his warm breath brushing her face.

"We aren't friends. I have no reason to all you anything else ," she hurled back taking pleasure in the fire that jumped into his eyes.

"Oh....we are going way past the friendship level before you leave here." He growled at her.

Why did she want to flirt with disaster? She knew that he was attracted to her. It would be dumb of her not to know from the way he looked at her. Why did she feel the need to push his buttons even further?

"You're so sure of yourself aren't you?" Daria asked trying to get the image of making love to him out of her head.

Sliding his hand through her hair, Lindow massaged her scalp with the tip of his fingers. "No...I'm not self-assured," he denied. "But I'm not going to fight what I see right before my eyes like you are." Turning her head, he ran the tip of his rough tongue along the outside of her ear.

Daria hissed in a deep breath between her two front teeth before her body collapsed against Lindow's. She couldn't concentrate on anything, but the feel of two warm hands easing her silk shirt out of her blue jeans. She wanted to tell him to stop, but she couldn't find the strength.

"Do you know how hard it was for me to keep my cool the first time I undressed you." Lindow questioned undoing the first button on her shirt. "I wanted to see you so bad without that peach bra, but I controlled myself."

Daria couldn't believe she was standing in the middle of the living room of a man she barely known a week allowing him to undress her. Her brothers would have a fit if they knew Detective Woods had kissed her more times that she could count.

"Stop...we can't do this." She whispered placing her hand on top of his as it moved from the second button to the third one. "I'm here to help find my cousin not get involved with you. Beside you have Jackie to fulfill any urges you might have," She mumbled turning away from him.

Lindow reached his hand out to touch Daria and let her know how wrong she was, but the sound of the doorbell stopped him. "Saved by the bell," he uttered walking away he went to answer the door.

Staying in the living room Daria tried to get her body back under control. Detective Lindow Woods was just too damn fine for his own good. She made a mental note not to let his lips anywhere near her weakening body.

She heard Lindow's voice in the hallway along with another one that sounded somewhat familiar. Wanting to know who Detective Woods conned into watching her for the night she eased into the hallway and bit the inside of her mouth to keep from cursing.

After she got her emotions back under, Daria glared at the unwanted guest, "Please tell me this is a horrible joke," she hissed placing her hands on her hips.

Chapter Seven

Dark brown eyes flickered over her once with distaste before they focused their attention back on Lindow. "Am I interrupting something?" A.J. asked jerking his head back toward Daria. "If the two of you were busy I can come back."

Lindow looked back at Daria and noticed her shirt was still open revealing a leopard print bra which looked so tantalizing next to her rich brown skin. "No, you weren't bothering us at all" He lied wishing A.J. wasn't in the room with them. "Daria was on her way to her bedroom to change clothes when the doorbell rung. "Weren't you?"

Daria threw him a look that could have melted butter and then started to button her shirt back up. "Yeah...that's what I was going to do."

"See, nothing is going on here that shouldn't be," Lindow muttered as he watched her leave the hallway and head for her bedroom. He waited until her bedroom door closed before he refocused his attention back on A.J.

"Thanks for doing this on your day off." Lindow uttered patting his partner on his the shoulder. "I can't let her come to the station with me. She would drive the captain up the walls with all of her questions."

A.J. took off his jacket and handed it to him. "The only reason I agreed to baby sit your girlfriend is so I can watch the basketball game on your big screen television."

Lindow hung up A.J.'s coat in the closet behind him then turned back around. "Daria.... Ms. Jacobs," he quickly corrected when his partner gave him that I-told-you-so look, "is only a witness to a crime. She doesn't even consider us friends."

"Sure....that's why she is staying at your house instead of a hotel." A.J. snickered under his breath.

"She got attacked the last time I placed her in a hotel room. I don't want that to happen to her again. We can't be positive that Marcus and Gary wouldn't hurt her or worse."

Lindow stared at his partner of the past seven years and wondered what was going on in that head of his. Would he really take care of Daria while he was gone? Or would he piss off Daria so bad that she would stay in her room for the rest of the night. He hoped that he didn't make a mistake by inviting his buddy over here.

"Don't worry I'll keep an eye on her." A.J. sighed going past him into the study off to the side of the house where the big screen television was. Lindow had worked a lot of overtime to be able to purchase that baby.

Lindow followed behind his friend and watched as A.J. hurry over to his favorite tan recliner and took a seat like he owned the place. Picking up the remote, he clicked through the channels under he found the one the basketball game was on.

"You aren't going to stay glued to this game and not check on Daria are you?" he questioned moving to stand by the side of the chair. Sometimes A.J. could be a very disrespectful when it came to a person he didn't like. He never saw a lot of it on the force, but every once and a while it would pop out.

A.J. twisted around in the chair and pinned him with a bored look. "No, I won't forget to check on your woman."

"How many times do I have to tell you that she isn't my woman?"

"You can tell me that until you're blue in the face, but it doesn't mean that I'm going to believe you," A.J. laughed turning back to the television as the teams came out on the court.

"Well you should," Lindow snapped trying to make his mind believe it as much as A.J. He had to start paying more attention to this case and less to the tempting woman in the bedroom next to his.

"While I'm gone try and see if you can make Daria eat something. I know she hasn't eaten anything all day and it's almost supper time."

"I didn't realize this was a daycare. Do I need to help her down for a nap too?" A.J. muttered under his breath.

"Not if you don't want to end up with a black eye, you'll stay away from anything that deals with Daria and a bed," Lindow retorted as he went out of the room and moved towards the front door.

"I knew that there was something going on between the two of them." He heard A.J. complain behind him.

"I heard that."

"Good....now maybe you'll stop lying about it," A.J. said before he turned up the basketball game.

Lindow snatched his leather jacket off the back of the couch and slid his arms into it. He adjusted it over the straps of his holster then moved in the direction of Daria's bedroom. He had to get a few things straight with her before he left. He only hoped she would listen to him.

He paused outside the door as he head soft music coming from the other side. Lindow knocked once and waited.

"Come in." A soft voice whispered a few seconds later.

Pushing the door he walked inside and froze in the middle of the floor as he watched Daria's breast pushed against the thin fabric of the baby blue shirt as she twisted her hair at the back of her neck. Daria looked at him and he saw the desire appear in her eyes before she glanced away.

"I thought you had already let for the station," she muttered moving around the room so she wouldn't have to look at him again.

"No....I'm going to leave after I talk to you." He liked how the top and matching jogging pants make Daria sexier. Most women couldn't carry off that comfortable look, but she did adding a little class to it.

"What do you want to talk to me about?" she questioned folding back the covers on the bed making his mind wander to things that it shouldn't.

"I don't want you to get into an argument with A.J. while I'm gone. The two of you may not get along, but I asked him over here to protect you and he'll do that."

Daria glanced at him from her position by the bed and thin line of sweat started to slide down his back. Damn he wanted that woman more than anything in the world. "Did you give him the same lecture before you came into my room? Or am I the only one that gets this privilege?"

"No, my little spitfire I talked to my partner before I saw you and he agreed to be on his best behavior." Lindow chuckled when Daria gave him a disbelieving look.

"Hmmm...sure he did." She whispered tossing some extra pillows into the chair next to the bed. "He hates me and you know it."

"Hates is such a strong word to use." Lindow uttered. "He isn't fond of you at the moment. Maybe after tonight the two of you can form a friendship."

Daria snorted, "Friendship?" She shook her head. "I don't think we'll ever have a friendship. The best you can hope for is an understanding."

"If you willing to have an understanding with my partner then what are you saving for me?" he questioned coming across the room.

"I'm not saving anything for you, Detective, but a thank you for when you find my cousin safe and alive," Daria replied standing her ground by the side of the bed.

Lindow had to give her credit. His little spitfire's pulse was racing a mile a minute at the side of her neck. Her eyes were filled with such a burning desire that he wanted to toss her back on the bed and forget all about how he volunteered to work some extra hours on the Wells' case. But Daria was standing in front of him like she wasn't feeling a thing for him.

"You keep telling yourself that because I'm going to take great pleasure in proving you wrong," he mumbled before planting a quick kiss on her mouth. He ended the kiss the second he felt Daria's smooth hand touch the side of his cheek. "As much as I would love to continue this little verbal foreplay I'm needed at the station." Unable to resist the pull of her, he planted another quick kiss on her mouth and went out the door.

"Be careful." Daria whispered at his back missing the smile it brought to his face.

A.J. sat in the chair totally engrossed in the basketball for about a half and hour before he finally decided to recognize that Daria had even entered the room. Turning down the volume some he glanced over at her standing by the window.

"Move away from there." He sighed. "I don't need you getting shot and Lindow blaming me for not keeping a close eye on you."

Daria stormed away from the window and sat in a chair as far as she could get away from him. "Why are you here? I know what we feel for each other is mutual."

Picking up the remote he waved it toward the game. "For a big screen television I can deal with anything, and that means even you."

"So, you really aren't here to watch me. I can leave anytime that I want to." Daria questioned.

A.J. tried not to have a nasty comment back, but he couldn't help it. Daria Jacobs just rubbed him the wrong way. "Yes...I'm here to watch you and if you don't stop acting like a spoiled brat. I'll lock you in that room until Lindow comes back. He said I had to watch you not have a conversation with you."

"You don't have the power to do that to me," she hurled back.

"I've the power to do anything that I want because my partner left me in charge of you." A.J. glanced back at the game when he heard the crowd going wild over a shot that he missed. "Woman....can't you go and find something to do and stop making me miss the game."

"Not a problem. There are some things that I want to do in my room anyway." Daria jumped up out of her seat as he looked back at the ballgame.

Easing into her room Daria closed the door behind her and hurried over to the dresser by the window. Picking up the phone, she punched in a few numbers and gave the information to the man on the other side. Hanging up the phone, she snuck over to her bedroom window and pushed it open.

She would have loved to gone out the front door, but A.J. would have stopped her in a hot second, so this was her only other option. It kinda of reminded her of when she was a teenager and she snuck out to get some extra studying done at the library.

She looked back over her shoulder one last time before she climbed out and took off across the yard to the corner.

Chapter Eight

Lindow sat back in the leather chair and tapped the end of his pen against the edge of his desk. He wondered where in the hell Ronnie Wells was hiding out. There was a lot of places that a young attractive boy like Ronnie could find to hide, but after a while someone usually got tired sneaking around and showed their face.

However, he had searched several known drug handouts after he left his house and Ronnie wasn't in any of them. He was starting to believe the boy wasn't alive anymore, but he wanted him to be for Daria's sake. She loved her younger cousin like a mother lion protecting her baby cub.

She didn't want to believe that Ronnie wasn't dealing drugs, but he had proof. Right before his hit and run trial Ronnie was photographed taking a thick brown envelope from Rex Staples, a big time drug dealer in the area.

He was going to give her the information when he called her before the trial. But she blew him off and he kept the information to himself. A.J. might be right and Daria was helping out her cousin, so he couldn't let her know about everything just in case he had to use the information in the future.

Rex just got released from prison a little over a year ago after serving an eight year jail sentence for peddling drugs twenty yards from an elementary school. Lindow tried his hardest to get that low life more years added on to his sentence. A third grader died after he was seen talking to Rex, but the judge said there wasn't enough proof that Rex had anything to do with it.

Now Rex was out ruling the streets, corrupting the minds of new minors. A guy like that needed to stay in prison for a long time without the possibility of parole. If he had anything to say in it, the key to his prison cell would disappear and never be found again.

Staples was bad news for anyone who crossed his path and he hoped that Daria's cousin hadn't stolen money from Rex. But if he had, it would only be a matter of time before Rex found him. After that, the Ronnie Wells that Daria loved so much wouldn't be around anymore. She would be lucky if the cops found a body at all.

Standing up, Lindow walked over to his Captain's office door and knocked once. After hearing a muffled "Come in." He opened the door and quickly closed it behind him. He took a seat in the front of the desk and waited for his boss to get off the phone. He wished that he had more news to give his boss, but he didn't

Hanging up the phone Captain Robert Bell took off his glasses and pinched the bridge of his nose then placed them back on his face.

"Please tell me you have some news on the Wells boy," Captain Bell's gruff voice exclaimed due to years of smoking.

"No...I searched again in some of the local drug hangs out, but none admitted to seeing him," Lindow answered.

"Do you think they were lying?" Captain Bell questioned.

"I honestly don't know. You know most of them get their drugs from Rex, so I don't think they're going to sell him out to us."

"I don't care what you have to do. We need to find that Wells boy. He's the only person that can connect Rex and that third grader who died from that heroine overdose."

Lindow sat forward in the chair and stared at his boss. "I still don't understand why no one knew about Ronnie before Rex's case went to court."

"The prosecutor didn't bother to look for any new information after the judge stopped with that part of the case. They wanted Rex to do jail time for drugs and he signed that plea deal."

Lindow jumped up from the chair and paced around his boss's office. "I can't believe that they let him get away with murder. Do you know how hard it was to look that kid's mother in the eye and tell her Rex wasn't going away for her son's death?"

"Calm down...we can still get him if we find Ronnie and get him to testify for us." Captain Bell stared across the room at Lindow wearing a hole in his carpet. "Has his cousin provided any new information? I was positive that he would try to contact her."

"Daria wouldn't tell me if he had or not. All she does is defy me at every turn, but Rex must be scared that Ronnie will too, because he sent Marcus and Gary after her. I know they haven't stopped trying to get her."

"I agree with you there," Captain Bell said. "Rex is just waiting for another opportunity to snatch Daria and make her talk. You really need to keep a close eye on her."

"I'll do the best I can, but if she doesn't stop trying to play Little Miss Detective I'm not going to be able to help her," Lindow complained retaking his seat. "I didn't trust her to stay in the house alone while I came to work."

"Yeah...I heard that you talked A.J. into stay with her," Captain Bell laughed. "I thought the two of them didn't get along."

Lindow smirked. "They can't stand each other. Daria is a little too outspoken for A.J. He likes his women a little more submissive plus he thinks Daria is helping Ronnie hide from us."

The laughter vanished from Captain Bell's tone at his comment. "Do you think she is?"

"I don't know if Daria is or isn't. I can honestly say that I don't think she knows where he is right now."

"And if she finds out will she tell you."

Lindow wished that he could say yes, but he knew that he wasn't positive what Daria would do if she found Ronnie before they did. He just hoped that Rex didn't find both of them before he could help either one of them.

"No....I think Daria would try to be Ronnie's protector and sneak him back home with her."

"You have to make sure that doesn't happen," Captain Bell told him.

"I know," Lindow agreed.

Daria pulled money out of her jogging pants pocket and paid the cab driver after he parked in front of the abandoned warehouse. Getting out of the taxi, she moved back as he drove off after giving her one last look. She wrapped her arms around her waist and walked towards the door at the end of the building.

She remembered coming to this place and she hoped she was right about her instincts. She couldn't believe she didn't remember this place until now. She tested the door to make sure it was unlocked and she hurried inside closing it behind her. She blinked a couple of times getting her eyes use to the darkness of the room.

The cab driver had circled the block three times before he finally decided to drop of her off. But that was only after she promised not to mention he was the one that brought her here. It wasn't the best part of town and she could understand that he didn't want to be blamed if something happened to her. She had agreed to his demands and now here she was.

"Ronnie, I know that was you I saw outside Detective Woods' window. I know you're in here. This is the place you told me about during the trial. With everything that has been going on I forgot about it until now," Daria yelled walking around the cold, semi-dark warehouse. If the lights from the street weren't peeking in through the cracks in the window she wouldn't be able to see at all.

"You know that I've always been there for you even when we were kids, but if you want my help now, you need to stop hiding," she yelled again going toward the back of the building.

"How do I know you won't turn me into that detective?" A voice muttered from somewhere in the darkness of the room.

"Did I ever tell dad about how you were the one that ruined his favorite shirt by adding beach to the washing machine?" she asked looking into the direction Ronnie's voice came from.

"No....you didn't tell on me," Ronnie answered in a small voice more like a little kid, not a criminal on the run. He sounded a little closer to her this time.

"Well...the same thing goes here. I'm your lawyer, but we are family and right now you're coming first with me. I wouldn't let Detective Woods or anyone else hurt you," Daria promised trying to get through to him.

"Why are you here looking for me? I thought you would still be pissed that I didn't go back to college like you wanted."

"I'm here because Marcus and Gary came to me looking for you," Daria answered, her eyes trying to find Ronnie in the darkness.

"Oh, did they hurt you? I didn't think it would go this far," Ronnie stated.

Daria placed her hands on her hips and moved to the part of the warehouse that had the most light. She was getting tired of this game. "Ronnie, either you come out where I can see you or I'm out of here. Do you know how much trouble I can get in if Woods or anyone finds out I'm here with you?" she questioned tired of Ronnie and his problems with the law lately.

"I'm sorry I got you into all of this, Cuz." Ronnie whispered coming into the light from Daria's left.

Twirling around, Daria gasped at the sight of her overly thin cousin standing behind her in the dimly light room wearing a torn white t-shirt and stained jeans. She tried her best to ignore the odor coming for his body. It didn't look like he had taken a bath in weeks. She wasn't able to get a good look at him back at house. *Where in the world had he been the past six months that he hadn't gotten anything to eat?*

"Oh my God, Ronnie," she whispered rushing toward her cousin, but he held out his hand holding her at bay.

"Don't touch me. I haven't bathed in weeks, so I don't know what's living on my body."

"I don't care about that." Daria argued taking another step toward him.

"Well...I do," Ronnie snapped back at her. "The only reason I took a chance coming to that Detective's house was to see you," he admitted rubbing his hands up and down his arms.

"I found out you were there from one of my friends. Marcus and Gary won't bother you there. I know there are tough, but they aren't crazy enough to break into a cop's house."

Daria noticed how Ronnie was shaking a little and seemed unfocused. She didn't know how she could help him if he was all strung out.

"Are you on drugs?" she questioned trying to sneak a glance at his arms for needle marks.

"Hey....I'm not doing drugs, Daria." Ronnie groaned scratching his head. "I just haven't eaten any food in a while," he groaned. "See how you act when you can't remember your last meal."

She felt her heart breaking for her cousin. Ronnie didn't deserve this. He was such a happy little boy, but he always wanted to find his parents. She was only six years older than Ronnie, however she felt more like his mother than cousin.

"Let me go and get you something to eat. I saw a convenience store at the end of the corner. It will only take me a few minutes."

"No! I don't want to involve you any more than I have," Ronnie repeated, but she could see the excitement in his eyes at the possibility of a hot meal.

"Don't argue with me. I'll be right back," Daria promised as she ran for the door. "Close this door behind me and lock it if you can. I'll knock twice when I get back and then you let me in." She opened the door and peeked her head out making sure the coast was clear. Daria stood at the door until she heard the lock turn then she took off to find some food.

"What in the hell are you talking about?" Lindow snapped standing in the opened bedroom door to Daria's room. He glared over at A.J. who was next to him. He was able to get a stack of paper work done at the station because he thought Daria was home safe with A.J. and in reality she wasn't. "Where in the hell did she go?"

"I don't know where she went to or how long she has been done," A.J. whispered then he took a step back from the glare in his best friend's eyes.

"You shouldn't have upset her," Lindow muttered. He moved across the room and stood in front of the open window. "I can't believe you let her crawl through the window." Lindow took off his leather jacket and flung it down on the bed. "God, you supposed to be my partner! I should be able to trust you to handle a woman half your size." He complained spinning back around.

"You can't control her either," A.J. flung back.

"We aren't talking about me here. Daria was under your protection and you failed to keep her safe. Do you know that we're just assuming that she went out this window by herself? Marcus, Gary or anyone else could have snatched her through it."

"That didn't happen."

"How would you know that?" Lindow exploded it. "You were too busy enjoying my big screen television to pay attention to my witness. You know without her we don't have a good chance of finding Ronnie." He sighed trying to calm down his attitude. "Why do you think Marcus and his two cent sidekick are after her too?"

As soon as Daria came back from where ever she went to they would have a long talk about this latest stunt.

"Man, I'm sorry that I didn't pay better attention," A.J. apologized like he was truly sorry for his mistake. "Let me help you go and look for her," he offered again.

"No....I don't want you to do that," Lindow replied with a quick head shake. "Why don't you go back to the station and see if any new information about Ronnie has come up?"

"Okay, I'll call you if I find out anything." Brushing past him A.J. picked up his jacket off the couch and went out the front door closing it softly behind him.

Lindow was pissed that his partner allowed Daria to maybe sneak out into the night right under his nose. *Damn it*! He wasn't going to let A.J.'s bad attitude put his life or Daria's into jeopardy. Tomorrow at work he would'have a long talk with A.J. Hell, he was even thinking about asking Captain Bell for a new partner. He knew it might he hard to get one after being with A.J. for seven years, but it was a thought running to his mind after what happened tonight.

Chapter Nine

Daria sat on the warehouse floor and watched her cousin Ronnie devour his fourth piece of chicken. She was so happy that the store at the corner sold a little bit of everything from fresh food, snacks to t-shirts and knock off jeans.

She was able to get Ronnie some clean clothes, food and a small box of carrot cakes. She wouldn't have been able to do any of this, if she hadn't shoved that extra money into her pocket before climbing out the window.

Daria studied Ronnie as he shoved one of the mini carrot cakes into his mouth. She had to find out what was going on, so she could help him out of this new trouble that he was in. There had to be a good reason that Marcus and Gary were looking for him that didn't involve stolen money or drugs. Ronnie wouldn't disappoint her family like this not after all what they did for him from birth until now.

"Please tell me why you're hiding in this cold dark building?" she asked grabbing a chicken leg out of the box. Taking a small bite, she waited for some kind of response from Ronnie. She prayed it was what she wanted to hear.

Ronnie stopped reaching for a drumstick and gawked at her. "He'll kill me if I tell."

Finally! She thought they were getting some where. "Who will?"

"Don't ask me if you don't want to get yourself placed on the hit list with me," Ronnie tossed back. "The guy who's after me doesn't want me to talk and he'll do anything to keep me quiet."

Daria finished off her leg and reached for a wing while trying to think of who Ronnie was so terrified of. During the trial he had given he a list of criminals that wanted him to be sent away. Marcus and Gary had been on that list, but they weren't powerful enough for Ronnie to be this scared of.

Pulling the wing apart, she took a small nibble then glanced down at her watch and almost choked. She had been gone for almost two hours. Tossing the chicken back into the box, Daria jumped up from the floor. Detective Woods was going to kill her. There was no way he wasn't back from the station by now.

"I need to leave," she told Ronnie digging her cell phone out of the side pocket of her jogging pants. "I didn't realize I had been gone for so long. Punching in the number for the cab, she gave the guy the information he wanted and hung up.

Ronnie stood up beside her and wiped his hands down the sides of his stained jeans. "Thanks for the new clothes," he said nodding toward the clothes next to the extra box of chicken. "I'll go to the gas station up the street and use their bathroom to clean up."

Daria didn't want to leave Ronnie in a place like this. He shouldn't have to be hiding out like this. She was positive that he hadn't done anything wrong with Marcus and Gary. Her cousin deserved a chance to clear his name and she wanted to give him that chance.

"Please come with me back to Detective Woods'. He really isn't that bad. He'll listen to your side without judging you." She insisted wanting to get through to Ronnie before it was too late.

"No.....you know I don't like cops and Woods isn't any different," Ronnie disagreed.

"You're wrong," she countered. "He isn't like the rest of them. Lindow is a good guy." Daria stated not realizing she used Detective Woods' first name.

"You need to go outside so that cab will stop for you. They don't come into this part of town a lot after dark." Ronnie stated shoving her to the door.

"Don't you dare leave this warehouse," she told Ronnie. "I'll try to come back with more clothes and food later." Opening the door, Daria went outside at the same time the cab pulled up. She hurried and got inside the vehicle then waved good-bye to Ronnie before he went inside the building

All the lights were off inside the house even his car wasn't in the driveway, she couldn't believe her luck as she hurried down the sidewalk. Maybe she had worried about this all for nothing because he wasn't even home from the station. Daria paused in the middle of the yard and peeked around the tree she had seen Ronnie at earlier.

She wasn't going to get a lecture from Detective Woods because he wasn't home and maybe if she prayed hard enough he wouldn't be back until tomorrow. Moving quickly from behind the tree Daria tried to hurry across the grass back to the side of house without being spotted by the neighbors. It wouldn't do any good if one of them called the cops on her.

Her mind did sort of wonder where A.J.'s car was, but after the way he treated her that thought didn't stay long. She was halfway across Detective Woods' yard when all the lights came on in his house including the front porch. The front door was flung open and Lindow's towering body filled the doorway, Daria was too stunned to move from her frozen spot in the middle of the yard.

"There's no need for you to try to sneak back in after being gone for hours," Lindow snapped stepping back from the doorway. "You can come on in right through the front door." He moved back allowing her access to his home.

Her feet carried her inch by inch to the open door and she tried not to notice the veins popping out of Detective Woods' forehead. He was beyond mad! Daria didn't know if she could take another long '*Where have you been*?' speech tonight. It had been a long night and she wanted to get to bed.

"What makes you think I was trying to sneak in?" she questioned sliding past Detective Woods' fit body. The clean fresh scent of him almost made her want to get a closer smell of what he was really wearing.

"I was watching you through the window," Lindow muttered slamming the door shut. "I know the look of someone trying to hide something."

Daria couldn't control her tongue quick enough from saying the words she wanted to keep down. "How dare you say that to me? I've nothing to hide from you!"

"Not even going to visit your cousin Ronnie in the middle of the night?" Detective Woods questioned.

Blinking a couple of times, Daria wondered did Detective Woods know where Ronnie was or was he just picking her to find out?

"I don't know what you're talking about," she answered as she tried to leave the room. She only moved two steps when Detective Woods twirled her back around to face him.

"Don't lie to me, Daria," he pleaded. "I'm here to help you. Why can't you understand that?" Lindow's eyes searched Daria's face She wanted so bad to ask him for help, but she couldn't break her promise to Ronnie.

"How can I trust you when you wanted to send my cousin to jail to teach him a lesson?" Daria questioned. "What kind of help do you call that?"

"The kind of help you should have agreed to and your cousin wouldn't be in the trouble that he's in," Lindow argued back. "If Ronnie gets hurt or turns up dead it will be your fault."

How dare he say that? He didn't know a thing about how much she wanted this chaos to disappear about Ronnie.

"So you do know where he is?"

She wasn't about to let this man in front of her break her down about Ronnie. If he wanted to find her cousin then he would have to do it without her help. How could she know Ronnie's problems wouldn't get worse if she involved him?

"I'm not going to answer that question again, Detective." Daria replied proud of the calmness in her voice. "Now, I'm going to bed and I'll see you in the morning." She turned and walked slowly to her bedroom with the hope the subject would be dropped.

"Daria, I'm not finished talking to you. Come back here. We still need to discuss the sneaking out problem you have. I won't allow you to do that anymore."

"Try and stop me," she threw back at him. Daria opened the bedroom door walked in and closed it behind her without looking back.

"Don't worry my little spitfire," Lindow muttered at the closed door. "I've got just the thing to keep you from wandering away from me."

Chapter Ten

After finishing her shower Daria pulled on her favorite black nightgown and lay down on her stomach in the middle of her bed. She reached for the thick manila envelope she placed on the bed earlier. Flipping it open she dug out the white slip of paper that had all the names Ronnie told her about during his trial.

Someone on this list had to be the person that wanted her cousin dead and she would find out who it was without or without Lindow's help. Brushing her hair away from her cheek she took a better look at the list.

1. Ja'coby King – small time drug dealer.
2. Marcus "Guns" Mitchell deals with mostly guns and drugs part time.
3. Gary Nolan – charged with attacks some women never convicted, partnerswith Marcus.
4. Bo Robinson – disappeared right before Ronnie's hit and run trail. Rex "pretty boy" Staples' partner in crime.
5. Rex "Pretty Boy" Staples – Big time drug dealer. Sent away right before Ronnie's trial on plea bargain deal, might have ties with foreign drug dealers.

She really wanted Marcus and Gary to be behind the fear in her cousin's eyes, but the two of them weren't big time enough. She would bet her law degree that those two were working for one of the other people on this list.

What had Ronnie gotten himself into that he had a paid hit out on him? Why hadn't Marcus and Gary shown their faces in a couple of days? What did Ronnie know about one of these men on this list that he wasn't telling her?

A knock on the bedroom door almost made her jump out of her skin.

"Come in," she whispered, quickly shoving the paperwork into the folder on her bedspread and underneath her pillow. She wasn't going to share this list yet with Lindow. He would want to a copy so he could investigate it for himself while keeping her out of it. She was still Ronnie's lawyer and had a right to look into some of these people herself.

The doorknob turned and Lindow's body filled the doorway. He was wearing a pair of gray sweat pants with a matching t-shirt stretched to the seams by all his muscles pushing against the fabric.

"I saw a light underneath the door, but I had to make sure you hadn't run off again," he said blocking the doorway as his obvious sex appeal filled the small room. His eyes stared at the parts of her breasts exposed by the position she was in on the bed. The predatory look sent a sudden awareness of him throughout her body.

Daria quickly scurried off the bed and pulled down her nightgown. "Yes, I'm here and you can leave," she replied.

"What are you working on?" Lindow asked. I know you're doing something in here. It's not like you not to be up to something you don't want me to know about."

"Nothing important," she lied as Lindow moved away from the door further into the room to her.

She just noticed then that his dark hair was wet like he had just taken a shower. The clean scent of his body made her own body pulsate for his touch. Daria shook her head a couple of times to get rid of the thoughts, but they stayed with her.

"Do you know how unbelievable you look in that nightgown?" Lindow questioned as his eyes lingered on the rise and fall of her breasts. "Did you wear it so I could strip it from that sinful body of yours?" He took another step closer to her and she took two steps back.

"No," she gasped caught up by the heat in his green eyes.

"Are you sure that you didn't?" Lindow asked her again, "Because that's the third item on my Daria-to-do-list."

She quickly closed her eyes and prayed for strength at the mention of that damn list again. Opening her eyes, she was taken back by how close Lindow was to her now. Not quite close enough to touch her skin, but close enough for her undersexed body to recognize the presence of his.

"Third item," she whispered trying her best to ignore the large tent forming in front of Detective Woods' pants. Damn the thought of what was underneath his clothes made her body ache. What would happen if he suddenly stripped out of all of his clothes right here right now?

"Yeah....the third item," he growled, eliminating the small gap that separated their bodies. "You surely didn't think I only had two items on my list?" Lindow inquired as the pad of his thumb brushed across her hard nipple through the nightgown.

Daria's hands shot out and grabbed Lindow's upper arms to keep from collapsing at his feet as a quick stab of pleasure raced through her body.

"I hadn't given it much thought," she moaned.

"Oh, you should my little spitfire," Lindow muttered as he lifted her up and placed her on the sturdy dresser behind them. "I add something new to my list every time I get a chance," he confessed as he pushed down the left strap of her nightgown exposing one of her breasts.

She heard a curse in the back of her mind as Lindow long fingers skimmed the apart around her nipple, but he wouldn't touch it. She was about to go crazy and he was playing with her.

"Please," she moaned.

"Please, what?" Lindow taunted brushing the side of her breast with his fingers.

"You know what I want," Daria moaned pressing her breast against Lindow's hands.

Emerald green eyes held her brown ones in an intense gaze without blinking. "Not until you do number one on my list."

Number one, she thought. What in the hell was number one again? Her mind couldn't focus through the sexual daze Lindow had her in.

Chapter Eleven

"Do you not remember number one, my little spitfire?" Lindow asked sliding the fingers from his free hand between her thighs. He slowly pushed her nightgown out of the way until it rested above her knees.

"Sure, I remember what number one is," Daria lied trying to scoot her lower body closer to his fingers. She could almost feel the brushing of his hands but not quite.

"Are you sure that you do?" he asked running one long finger down the front of her underwear causing her body to jerk under the light touch. "I don't like it when you lie to me," he muttered touching her with a second finger.

Daria bit her lip to keep from coming apart right there in front of him. "I'm pretty sure that I'll remember what number one was," She moaned.

Leaning forward, Lindow licked the tip of her ear with his tongue, "I need you to be more than pretty sure," he muttered sliding his two caressing fingers inside her underwear. "I can't do what you want me to until I get what I want." Moving his lips down her neck, he slowly licked his way down her chest until his mouth was positioned above her hard nipple.

"Think real hard I know that you'll recall the first number on my Daria-to-do list," he encouraged before he slid one thick finger inside her body.

She couldn't control the moan that shot out form her mouth as the feel of Lindow's hot finger inside of her. He wasn't moving it in and out of her body at all. It was just there taunting her making her want more and more of him.

Tiny beads of sweat started to cover her body as she fought the need to move her body against his hand. Why was she letting him do this to her? *You know why*, her mind taunted. *You want this man so damn bad that you can't see straight.*

"It's coming back to me," Daria whispered trying to fight down the need to move her body.

"Well, maybe I can help jog your mind a little more," Lindow growled sliding two more fingers inside her body as he licked at the sweat covering the top of her breasts.

"Oh, my god!" Daria screamed as three thick male fingers filled her body. "I remember what it was....You wanted me to call you....Lindow," she moaned.

"Very good, my little spitfire," Lindow muttered before pulled he hard nipple into his mouth and sucking hard.

Daria closed her eyes and fell back on the dresser as Lindow spread her thighs wider and stepped between them as his firm mouth and tongue worked on her breasts. She had never felt like this with another man before. The men from her past didn't make her want her to forget who she was and live for the moment. She raised her hand and pressed it to the back of Lindow's head and as he feasted on her body.

"No...." Lindow muttered against her body removing his fingers from her body and mouth from her breasts.

She rose up on her elbow and stared at model of perfection standing between her legs. "What are you saying no to?" Daria panted above her beating heart.

Lindow sat her up on the dresser and fixed her clothes. "I don't want to take you on a hard surface. I want to take you in my bed, so I can enjoy this body of yours as much as I want to all night long."

Before she could say a word, Lindow lifted her up into his arms and carried her through her bedroom door and into his. He placed her on the bed and quickly covered her body with his. "Do you know what I want to do to you?" he asked kissing the side of her neck.

"No...I don't have a clue." Daria breathed taking to catch her breath at the feel of Lindow's thick erection poking at her. She couldn't wait until they were naked and she to feel him inside of her.

Lindow raised her hands above her head and ran his fingers over her breasts and down the side of her hips. "I want to keep you in this bed all night long until you don't forget to call me Lindow or any endearment that you want. I'll accept anything but Detective Woods," he muttered.

"What if I don't want to call you Lindow anymore after tonight?" Daria teased.

Dark green eyes narrowed on her face before Lindow's mouth kicked up into a smile that made her insides sizzle with passion. "Then you'll have to get punished," he growled.

"What kind of punishment?" she joked back enjoying the game Lindow was playing with her.

Sexual interest lit up the beautiful eyes staring into hers and Daria found herself enjoying that look. "Do you really want to know?" Lindow's deep voice questioned. "You might not like it."

"I'm game for whatever you throw my way.....Detective Woods," Daria taunted knowing that would get a rise out of Lindow.

Mumbling something that she couldn't hear, Lindow caught her wrists in one of his large hands and held her captive. "Now remember this is what you said that you wanted," he muttered reaching for something behind her head.

A few seconds later, she felt something cool wrap around her wrists and close with a loud click. Rolling off the bed Lindow stood up beside her with a huge grin on his handsome face. Daria tried to move her arms but couldn't. What in the world had Lindow done to her? She twisted her head to the side a little and saw that he had handcuffed her to the bed.

"Get these things off me right now," she demanded pulling at her wrists.

"I thought you were game for anything I threw your way my, little spitfire." Lindow teased planting a kiss on her mouth then he moved away.

"I didn't mean that you could handcuff me to your bed," she snapped tugging at her wrists again. "I want you to let me up this second."

Lindow pulled the t-shirt over his head showing her a perfect washboard stomach with a light dusting of black hair. For a moment she forgot that she was pissed at the man standing in front of her and just enjoyed the sight of him.

"I can't do that," he sighed looking down at her in his bed. "I don't have to be at work until late tomorrow and I want to get a good night's sleep. I don't trust you to stay in your room all night." Lindow confessed coming around to the other side of the bed.

"You expect me to stay handcuffed to your bed all night long?!" Daria screamed giving her wrists another hard tug.

Lindow crawled in the bed beside Daria and covered them both with a light dark blue comforter. "Stop doing that or you'll bruise your pretty wrists," he mumbled kissing her by the side of her mouth. "Now, don't try anything funny and stop that twisting around. I need my beauty sleep."

Turning on his side, Lindow tucked his pillow under his neck and went to sleep ignoring the words of hate pouring from the gorgeous woman next to him.

Chapter Twelve

Daria snuggled closer to the warmth beneath her cheek. She hadn't felt this comfortable in such a long time. When was the last time she actually didn't want to get out of a bed? Whatever she was sleeping on was what made for her, because she fit against it perfectly. She stuck out her hand and ran it across something hard yet it was soft to her fingertips.

As much as she hated to she had to open her eyes and find out what was giving her such pleasure. Cracking open one eye, she stared at naked flesh covered by a dusting of dark hair.

What in the hell? She jumped up. Who in the hell was she in bed with? Her eyes swung open and scanned across the most flawless male face she had ever seen covered by a five o'clock shadow.

She frowned at the male who had the nerve to handcuff her last night to his bed after getting her all hot and bothered without doing a thing to relieve the ache he caused. Lindow was now on her *Most Wanted* list. He had no right to do those amazing things to her and then fall to sleep like nothing ever happened.

Daria raised her hand to punch Lindow hard upside his head when she realized that her hands were free. She swung her eyes behind her and noticed that the handcuffs where no where in sight. It was like all the events of last night never even happened. She was glad to be free, but she was still pissed that Lindow thought he had the right to do that to her.

How would he like it if she handcuffed him to her bed? Daria quickly shook the thought from her mind. With the way his mind functioned he would like it a little too much. Well, she couldn't let him get away with what he did to her. She had to find a way to get him back. She took another peek at his body and realized that he was still asleep. He did mention to her last night that he didn't have to be at work until late.

Daria wasn't about to let Lindow go back to work or get out of this bed without paying him back for what he did to her last night. She sat up in the bed and looked around the room. There had to be something in here at she could use against her. From her peripheral vision she noticed a pillow kicked on the floor. Perfect!

Reaching over the side of the bed, she picked it up and turned back around to Lindow. She couldn't believe she was about to do this, but it would teach him a lesson not to mess with her again. Lifting it above her head she swung it down hard hitting Lindow directly in the face.

"How dare you handcuff me to your bed last night!" She screamed swinging the pillow down for a second time. She was going for a third when the pillow was snatched from her hands and tossed back on the floor.

She was flipped on her back before the pillow even hit the ground. "My little spitfire, what in the hell do you think you're doing?" Lindow growled into her face.

Daria dropped her eyes down to his full bottom lip and wished that he would kiss her again. She wanted to feel the charge her body got when his mouth was pressed against hers.

"I'm paying you back fro the horrible way you treated me last night," she muttered struggling under Lindow's powerfully built body.

"I didn't treat you terrible, Daria," Lindow said tugging her arms above her head. "I only did what I had to do."

Hazelnut eyes grew darker as they glared at him. Did Daria know how difficult it was for him not to kiss her? Last night had been one of the hardest nights of his life. He had woken up with Daria next to him. She looked like a wet dream come true with both of her hands pulled over her head. Her breasts practically poured from that scrap of fabric she called a decent nightgown.

He lost track of how long he just lay next to her and watched her sleep after he removed the cuffs. He hated doing that to her, but he had to make sure she didn't do another two hour disappearing act on him.

"The only thing you had to do was leave me alone and I wouldn't had left," Daria groused twisting her enticing body under his. One more brush of that perfect breast against his already aroused body and Daria was in serious trouble. He was trying to be a good guy, but she was pushing him to his limits.

Lindow leaned his body down until he could feel Daria's sweet breath in his face. "Don't you know by now that I want to do more to you than just leave you alone?"

He wanted her to trust him enough to let him know what was going on with Ronnie. She hadn't mentioned it and he seriously doubted that she would, but he had a gut instinct that she had been with her cousin. When she going to realize he truly wasn't the bad guy here?

"Well, the only thing I want you do is get off me so I can get out of this bed," Daria complained pressing her body to his. "Let me up you're too heavy on me. Do you know how hard your body is?"

Lindow chuckled deep in his throat at the way Daria was trying to piss him off and avoid her attraction to him all at the same time. "No, I'm not too heavy for you because I'm not giving you all my weight, my little spitfire."

He whispered by Daria's ear. "I would never do anything to hurt you. You should know that by now. But I do know that there is one part of me that's really hard for you right now." Lindow muttered brushing his lower body to Daria's.

She gave her arms another tug in his, but he wasn't ready to let her go yet. He wanted to get a nice rest before work, but she wanted to play games in the bed. Now, that was something he would lose sleep for anytime of the day especially with the woman beneath him.

"I thought you were supposed to protect and serve," Daria's sweet voice mumbled at him.

Visions that shouldn't have entered his mind danced in his head. Nights filled with such passion that Daria wouldn't be able to leave his bed the next morning, let alone him. She would be so in love with him that the thought of going back to Washington, D.C. would never enter her mind.

"I'll serve you so many times in one night my little spitfire that I'll make you forget your own name," he promised by her ear. Lindow smirked as Daria's body flinched at his words. Her body wanted him and it was only a matter of time, plus one or two more things on the Daria-to-do list, and he'll have the woman he wanted for a lifetime.

Letting go of Daria's wrist, Lindow ran the palm of his hands down the side of her body. He enjoyed how the silky material of her gown moved over her skin. He caught her eyes with his and held them. Seconds seemed like hours before he finally asked the question swirling around in his mind.

"Are you ready to learn the next item on my list?"

Daria blinked at him a few times like she was trying to clear her head. "I don't care about that silly list of yours," she denied, but he felt how her body reacted when he brought up the list. She was dying to know what else he had planned for her.

"Now, for some reason I don't believe you," Lindow whispered touching his tongue to the pulse at the side of her neck.

"Well, I don't," Daria tossed back in that sultry voice he loved so much.

"Humor me."

Running her fingers through his hair, she searched his face with her eyes. "What do I get if I do?"

“Oh, I know that I can think of something that you'll like,” Lindow promised the woman beneath him.

“Oh, it better be real good,” Daria said stroking his lower back with her fingertips.

He grasped her hips yanking her to the part of him that was twitching with a need he had never known before in his thirty-seven years. It was killing him to play with her like this. “I can promise it's very hard and after I'm finished using it you'll feel real good for days.”

Daria panted at the heated sound of his words. She wanted to hear the next item on the Daria-to-do-list and he was going to tell her. He was only able to get part of it accomplished, but it wasn't anything to worry about. The other part would come true too.

“Number three was to wake up and find you naked in my arms,” He confessed.

“I'm not naked.”

“The day isn't over my little spitfire,” Lindow lowered his voice, so his words could caress over Daria's flesh making her want the same thing he did.

“You think you're talented enough to get me out of my clothes?” Daria teased him back.

“Well, if my memory is correct. I got pretty close last night,” he said, in a lower, huskier tone. “I know you remember that because I sure as hell do. Your body was so warm and tight around my fingers. I could have stayed inside of you for hours.”

“Stop, I don't want to hear anymore,” Daria mumbled twisting her head on his pillows.

“Why not? Am I wearing down that wall of yours? You know it would be so hot between us that even a cold shower afterwards wouldn't cool us off.” Lindow wanted Daria to say that she wanted him. He would keep tempting her with his list until she did.

“Stop...I don't want to hear anymore.” Daria begged shoving at his shoulders.

Lindow felt like a part of his heart had gotten ripped out of his chest as Daria's words washed over his body. Rolling out of the bed, he glared down at the temptress lying in his bed. She looked primed and ready for a good night of uncontrolled sex and she wasn't admitting to it. That pissed him off to know end. He was too old to play these hot and cold games with her.

“Until you're ready to at least admit you feel something for me. I'm finished with my Daria-to-do list. I can take that time and work on something else more constructive, like finding your cousin”.

“Once he’s found safe and alive. I can get what I need from him and toss you back on the first flight to Washington,” he snapped. His tone sounded steel. He turned on his heel and strode to the door, then went out to the bathroom down the hallway.

Chapter Thirteen

Daria didn't know how long she stayed in Lindow's bed before she finally rolled out of the bed. She couldn't believe that he stormed out of the room like that. He usually had something funny to say back to her or he tried to find another way to seduce her weak mind and body, but he didn't do any of that this time.

He actually went straight out the door and didn't even look back at her. Daria slowly made her way back to her own room. Once she got back inside she grabbed the manila folder from underneath her pillow and tossed it back into her briefcase. She didn't have time to worry about Lindow's feelings toward her now because focusing on Ronnie was more important. He was her family. She needed to find another way to communicate with him again.

The chances of him still being in that warehouse were slim to none, but she had to check it out and make sure he was okay. He was her responsibility since as long as she could remember. She was only six when her parent brought him into the house and the rest is history.

Quickly making up the bed, she dragged an outfit out of the closet and tossed it on the bed. Hopefully after taking hot shower and a good breakfast Lindow would be in a better mood. It crushed her when he said he wasn't going to work on his Daria-to-do list anymore. She wasn't about to admit it to him on the slim chance it would make him more conceited, but she loved when he popped out that list. She couldn't wait to find out what that sexy mind of his came up with next.

A sister could get use to having a sexy man like Lindow fantasizing about her. He was totally wrong for her in so many ways and then perfect for her in many more. She wished that she never made that rule not to date cops, because Lindow was one man that she wanted to get to know a whole lot better. The way his sex appeal made her pulse skip a beat made it almost illegal.

Shaking her head, she grabbed her robe off the bed and headed off for the shower hoping he was already finished and back in his room. She didn't have enough will power to resist a partially clothed Lindow. She sure in the hell wouldn't have enough strength of mind to resist a dripping wet, well-built with everything in the right place. She might turn last night's situation around and use those darn handcuffs on his sexy ass.

When she got to the middle of the hallway she noticed that Lindow's bedroom door was closed and the bathroom door was wide open. Daria didn't give herself enough time to ask why she was disappointed by that fact. Didn't Lindow tell her that he was tried of playing games with her? His only agenda was to find Ronnie and get her ass back home. She swallowed down some of the pain that his words still caused her. She wasn't about to force herself on a man who was no longer interested in her.

Walking into the bathroom, she closed the door and rested her back against it fighting off the sudden hot tears that clouded her eyes. Daria blinked several times to dry the tears and then headed to the shower hoping to be out before Lindow left for work. She wanted to go with him to the station. The police station would be the perfect place for her to research those men on her list some more. Without or without Lindow she was going to find out who was after her cousin.

Taking off the robe, she turned on the shower and got in hoping to wash all the thoughts that Lindow placed in her head out. She wouldn't let him stress her out today or any other day of the week. Tying the robe around her waist, she hurried from the bathroom back her bedroom. After getting dressed, Daria snatched her reading glasses off the dresser and stuck them on her face. She planned on doing a lot of reading today into the men on that list about Ronnie. There had to be a connection that she wasn't seeing and since Lindow was pissed at her, she knew he wasn't about to go out of his way to help her.

Going into the kitchen, Daria opened the refrigerator and looked for something to fix for breakfast. She couldn't go to the station and stay with Woods half the day without something in her stomach. When she didn't eat she became a major bitch and she couldn't afford to piss off Lindow anymore than he already was.

Grabbing the pitcher of orange juice off the top she placed it on the counter next to her. She was reaching for a package of bacon when she noticed the back door was opening next to her. Daria knew it wasn't Lindow because she heard him moving around in his room before she left hers. So, if her hunky detective was still in his room pissed off at her who in the hell was coming through the door?

Daria tried to calm down as vision of Gary and what he tried to do in the hotel came back to her. She didn't let him win that time and she wasn't going to let him win this time either. Ducking down she eased away from the refrigerator, spotting an empty pot on the stove she grabbed it.

She stayed calm as the person walked past her wearing a baseball cap and a tan jacket. It wasn't Marcus or Gary because the intruder wasn't black, but she wasn't taking any chances. It didn't mean the person looking for Ronnie hadn't sent someone else after her to finish the job.

Sneaking behind the person Daria raised the pot and brought it down toward the back of his head, but he moved before she made contact so it hit him on the shoulder.

"What the fuck!" The guy screamed as he turned around to her.

Eyes that looked more brown than green glared down at her from a six foot four inch frame. "Who in the hell are you?"

His voice was cold and exact causing her to take a step back although she held a weapon in her hand.

"Who in the hell are you?" she screamed raising the pot in her hand just in case. Before she knew what had happened the guy snatched the pot out of her hand and flung it across the room sending it crashing into the wall.

"Answer me," he growled "Where's Lindow?"

Daria spun around and tried running from the room, but a strong grip on her arm prevented her from moving anyway. She tried not to shake as the guy snatched off his hat and tossed it on the table. "Are you going to answer me?" he hissed between his teeth.

"Alec, let go of her arm right now," Lindow yelled coming into the kitchen. Rushing over to Daria he pulled the strong fingers from around her arm and sat her down at the table.

"Why are you defending this woman?" Alec mumbled rubbing the knot forming on the back of his shoulder. "She attacked me the second I walked into the house."

"What did you expected me to do when I saw the back door opening and a strange man walked through it?" Daria snapped back the second she regained her voice.

"Strange man?" Alec growled before he tossed a '*Can you believe this*' look at Lindow.

"Well, Daria does have a point." Lindow agreed going into his refrigerator looking for an ice pack for Alec. Finding one he tossed it across the room and Alec caught it in mid-air with his right hand. "She didn't have a clue."

Bracing his lower back against the counter Alec pressed the ice pack to his sore shoulder. "I didn't know I had to announce myself when I came into my own brother's house." Alec growled looking at Daria.

Daria swung her head over to Lindow then back over to Alec who hadn't taken his eyes off of her. She didn't miss the dislike in them. Well, it was more of a pissed look a man got when a woman got the better of him. "You have a brother?"

"Yeah..." Lindow muttered taking a seat next to her. "Guess... I forgot to mention that. We have been occupied with other things," he teased yanking at her ponytail.

She removed Lindow's hand from her hair and shot him a hard look and the devil had enough nerve to smile at her then wink. It was like his earlier rant in his bedroom never happened between them. God, she would never understand this man next to her and a part of her secretly loved it.

"Is there something going on here I should know about?" Alec asked cutting into their perfect world.

"No....there isn't," Daria muttered. She tried to move away from Lindow, but he wrapped his arms around her and placed her against his chest.

"Yes there is....but my little spitfire isn't ready to admit it yet," Lindow breathed by her ear. "She doesn't realize how patient I am. I might blow up once, maybe twice when I'm pushed, but I never give up on something that I really want."

Daria shivered as his words brushed over her body. How in the hell did she let herself get into the conversation with him and his brother? She wasn't going to sit her any longer and listen to this nonsense.

Pulling at Lindow long fingers, she moved them away from her body. "Don't listen to your brother. He doesn't know what he's talking about. I'm only here so he can help me find my cousin Ronnie."

Alec tossed the ice pack on the counter behind him and watched his brother reached for Daria again to only have his hands slapped away. "It looks like she doesn't want to be bothered with you big brother," he joked.

"She must be shy because you're here, because she didn't have a problem with my hands on her body this morning in bed," Lindow shot back.

Alec was glad that his brother had quick reflexes; because that was the only way he missed the hit up side the head Daria almost gave him.

"I was in your bed this morning because you handcuffed me there last night!" Daria hissed totally forgetting Alec was in the room with them.

"Handcuffed to the bed?" Alec chuckled. "Just what have you been up to?"

Lindow saw the hurt that started to glitter in Daria's dark eyes and knew he had taken his teasing too far. "Leave it alone Alec," he ordered looking at his brother. "Why don't you tell me why you're here?"

His brother took another look at Daria before he joined them at the table. "I wanted to invite you to the annual picnic that the fire station always has," Alec said. "I know last year you had to work and weren't able to make it. I thought you might come this year."

"I don't know," Lindow muttered sitting back in his chair. "I have to work on this case and I'm not getting any leads."

Alec stole another glance at Daria before he answered. "You can bring at date if you want."

Daria's head swung over and looked at him, but she didn't say a word.

Lindow did want to spend some time with Alec. They both worked so much that they didn't get a chance to hang out with each other. "I might stop by if I can get a certain someone to stop being mad at me and come." He nodded his head toward Daria who stuck her tongue out at him.

"You better be glad Alec's here, or I'd tell you the next item on my Daria-to-do list."

Lindow watched Daria's eyes start to burn with passion and another look that he couldn't quite read. Shit, why did Alec have to come from a visit now?

"I'm going to leave the two of your alone," Alec said getting up from the table. "I can see I came at a bad time."

"Ace, you don't have to leave. Nothing is going on here," Lindow said calling his brother by the name he gave him as a kid.

"You aren't even looking at me," Alec laughed as he open the kitchen door. "I think I'll come back another time when you aren't preoccupied with something...or should I say someone else." Alec studied his brother one last time before he went out the door closing it behind him.

"I'm sorry for the way I blew up at you earlier," Lindow told her contritely. He couldn't get over how bad he felt after he stormed out of his bedroom away from Daria.

"I'm the one who should apologize," Daria confessed staring at him. "I lied to your earlier."

Lindow knew he hadn't missed that look in her eyes a few minutes ago. There was a spark of some indefinable emotion in Daria's eyes and he wanted to find out what it was.

"What did you lie about?"

"I lied about...." The phone ringing cut off the rest of Daria was about to tell Lindow.

Chapter Fourteen

Lindow stared at Daria trying to block out the shrill of the phone. He couldn't believe when his little spitfire was about to confess to a lie she told him and the phone decided to ring. He could only imagine the words that were going to come out of those luscious lips of hers.

"Aren't you going to answer that?" Daria questioned when the phone wouldn't quit ringing in the background.

"No....let the answering machine pick it up." Lindow replied. "I want to know what you lied about."

"Well...I'm going to answer it. It could be some information about Ronnie." Daria jumped up to her feet, but Lindow waved her back down.

"Sit down. I'll get it," he relented standing up. Lindow cursed under his breath at the person's bad timing before he jerked the phone up to his ear.

"Woods....speak."

"Man, I thought you would never answer the phone," A.J. complained. "I don't have to ask who was keeping you busy."

"A.J. I know you didn't call here to criticize Daria, so what do you want?" Lindow snapped, still pissed at his partner and the incident with Daria. A.J. better be glad that she came back in one piece. Furthermore, if A.J. truly didn't calm down, he would ask Captain Bell for a new partner. His partner didn't know it, but he was walking a very thin line with him now.

"We pulled a body out of the water and it's pretty bad," A.J. informed him.

Lindow glanced at Daria and she was staring directly at him with that unblinking look of hers that he had come to love. But he couldn't let her see the reaction on his face if this turned out to be Ronnie. Picking up the phone, he carried it into the living room.

"Do you think it's Ronnie?" For Daria's sake he hoped that it wasn't. He knew she would blame herself.

"It's hard to tell because the face is totally beat up," A.J. informed him. "But the build is similar. We need Daria to come down and look at the body."

He didn't want to put Daria through that if he didn't have to, but he knew that it had to be done. If they body wasn't Ronnie, the station needed to start searching the other missing person's files and notify the correct family.

"All right, give me a half an hour and we'll be there." He hung up the phone before A.J. could say another word.

He tossed the phone of the table and ran his fingers through his hair. He needed to figure out a way to go and tell Daria about this. She loved Ronnie so much that if this really was him, it would kill her.

"That call was about Ronnie wasn't it?" Daria's soft voice questioned behind him, it wrapped around his heart making him care about her even more.

"I don't want you to get upset," Lindow softened his voice, turning to face her. "But a body was found this morning." He felt like a knife had been shoved in his heart at the sudden tears that filled Daria's eyes.

"It isn't Ronnie. I feel deep down that it isn't," she whispered, brushing away her tears.

Rushing across the room he wrapped his arms around Daria wanting to comfort her. He was pleased when she pressed her face to his chest instead of shoving him away. Maybe she was finally starting realize that he wasn't such a bad guy after all.

"I hope that it isn't Ronnie, Daria," he murmured rubbing her back. Lindow hated seeing the confident woman he was growing to care about in such pain. Daria stayed pressed against him for about five more minutes than she separated them.

"We better go. If it is Ronnie, I need to call and tell the rest of the family."

"Hey, how about we don't go down that road until we have to," he suggested brushing the tears off Daria's cheek with the pads of his thumbs.

"Okay." Daria touched his hand and squeezed it lightly before dropping it. She started to move around him, but he wrapped his hand around her upper arm and tugged her back to his body.

"You look like you need this."

"Need what?" she asked titling up head to stare up into his eyes. A painful expression covered her stunning face. Even when she was barely holding it together, Daria was the most exquisite woman he had ever laid eyes on.

He pressed her lips to hers, caressing her mouth more than kissing it. Lindow wanted to show Daria that he knew how to be gentle when the time called for it. It was a divine ecstasy when he kissed her. If Daria ever let him, he would kiss her each and every day of the week. Moving his mouth he pressed kisses around the side on her mouth working his way down her jaw. He would love to stay like this all day, but he couldn't and A.J. would only wait so long before he called again.

Raising his head he grinned down at the dazed woman in his arms. “I hate to say this, but we better go and see A.J. at the station.”

Nodding Daria moved out of his arms and picked up her purse off the couch and waited for him at the door. The soft look she sent him was almost enough to make him stay here at home with her wrapped back up in his arms.

However, he knew what he had to do. Lindow grabbed his jacket off the couch and slid it over his holster. He dug his car keys out of his pocket and made his way over to his beautiful house guest.

“Don’t worry, Ronnie isn’t dead. You would feel it if he was,” he assured opening the front door.

“I hope you’re right,” Daria responded following him out the door.

Chapter Fifteen

"Why in the hell did you throw his body in that lake?" Rex snapped. "If this comes back to me I'll make sure the both of you pay."

The two idiots in front of him glanced back and forth at each other before one of them got enough balls to finally speak up.

"You told us to ditch the body, so that's what we did," Gary tried to explain. "How did we know he'd be a floater?"

Gary ducked just in time to miss being hit in the head by a paper weight.

"Are you really this dumb, or are you acting this way to piss me off?" Rex growled slamming his hand back down on the table. "You dumped his body a mile from the police station."

"Boss, don't get upset," Marcus cut in. "We can fix this problem for you." He didn't want Rex "Pretty Boy" Staples pissed at him being the reason the police found the body.

Rex heard the fear in Marcus' voice and enjoyed the power he had in the room and the community. No one ever let the idea of crossing him enter their mind. They all know what happen if one of them did.

"Tell me have you fixed the Daria Woods problem. All I keep hearing about is our little freelance Nancy Drew and her investigation into where Ronnie is at."

Gary cut in before Marcus could stop him. "No... I think she's harder to get to now because she's staying with that detective," he complained. "He never lets her out of his sight."

"Why do you want to be alone with bitch again anyway? The last two times you were, she got the best of you," Rex laughed. He still thought it was funnier than hell that Gary let Daria shove a paperclip into his ear. He would never let that pint size nuisance get the best of him.

"I'm going to get her back," Gary assured him. "But now we need to get Woods and Bell off our backs."

"That's easier said than done," Marcus grumbled interrupting again. "An officer was just at my mother's house yesterday."

"She kept her mouth shut, didn't she?' Rex asked.

"Yes....after that one late night visit she received from you, my mother knows not to run her mouth," Marcus replied. He hated that Rex threatened his mother, but there wasn't a thing that he could do about it. Rex Staples wasn't a guy who made idle threats. He meant every word that came out of his mouth.

"Very good," Rex chuckled. "Nice lady that mother of yours; very hospitable. I enjoyed her so much I might have to visit her again real soon. She's a very good-looking woman."

Marcus was about to take a step towards his boss but Gary grabbed him by the arm. "Don't do it," Gary whispered out of the side of his mouth.

"You should listen to your friend there, Marcus," Rex chuckled, nodding his head in Gary's direction. "Have you forgotten what happened to the last guy that thought he could take me on?"

Marcus shook off Gary's touch and tried to calm down. He needed the extra money Rex was paying him to harass Daria Jacobs. As much as he wanted to throw a punch at Rex, he couldn't. His mother was one tough woman and knew how to protect herself it the opportunity ever came up.

"Sorry, boss I didn't mean any harm," Marcus apologized, glad that Gary stopped him in time from making a grave mistake.

"Don't worry about it. I give all my boys one lapse in judgment, but after that everything is laid out on the table," Rex replied with a smile but his eyes had a deadly glare. "However, if you think about confronting me again, I'll make sure your entire family pays dearly. First, I'll start with your sexy fifteen-year-old sister and end with your mother."

Marcus had heard in passing how Rex had taken revenge on some of his enemies. He had taken the younger victims and pushed them on the street, making them sell his drugs.

He didn't want that life for his mother and baby sister, so he would focus himself to keep his temper down. Because after what just happened, he already had a strike against him in Rex's book and that wasn't a good place to be.

"I apologize again, Mr. Staples. I swear to you it won't happen again."

"Very well.... Marcus," Rex sighed tired of hearing the young man beg and kiss up to him. He never had been fond of Marcus and only hired him because Gary recommended him. Now he was beginning to think that Marcus was becoming a problem he might have to get rid of.

Standing up he pulled his tailored silk suit jacket together and buttoned it up. He hated cleaning other people's errors up, but it seemed like this morning he was going to have to. So, he guessed a little trip was in his future.

The two dummies in front of him better hope this worked, because if it didn't, one of them was going to get an ass kicking from one of his bodyguards. Rex moved around the desk and checked his reflection in the mirror. He couldn't go out and not live up to his pretty boy name.

"Don't go anywhere. Stay here until I get back," Rex ordered heading for the door.

"Where are you going?" Marcus asked him fear in his voice.

A wolfish smile pulled at the corner of Rex's mouth. "Stop worrying Marcus, I'm not going to visit your family. They are safe-for now." Rex chuckled from the doorway, but he suddenly spun around and pinned Marcus with a stare that froze him in place. "However, if you questioned me again about where I am going, you might not be so lucky," Rex snapped then went out the door.

Outside, Rex stood and looked around the upscale neighborhood that he lived in and smiled to himself. Oh, he knew that everyone around him knew what he did to afford a place like he had, but none of them would dare turn him in to the cops. They all valued what they had too much to sell him out especially to those two detectives.

Did those idiots think he didn't see them cruising the area looking for any signs of his drug ring? Well, he wasn't born yesterday and they would never find out exactly where all of his drugs houses were located. Sure, they closed down one of them while he was in prison, but that was then and this was now.

He was back in full power, and nothing or no one was going to stand in his way of achieving his ultimate dream of being the only drug king here in town. That was the main reason he had to find a way to get little Ms. Washington, D.C. to go back where she came from.

Rex hated to admit it but the Jacobs' chick was a whole lot stronger and brighter than he thought she was. Most women after having two rounds with Marcus and Gary would have hightailed it back to the cushiony law job and forget all out their wayward cousin, but not her. She was like a hungry dog with a bone and it had to stop before she got too close and ruined his business.

Tossing up his head at his driver sitting inside his car parked at the curb, he waited while the man hurried out of the car, then opened the back door for him. Any other time he would have fired the idiot on the spot for not having the door open as soon as he came outside. But he was in a forgiving mood today because he had more important things that needed to be taken care of.

Getting inside the car he waited until his driver closed the door and got behind the wheel before he told him where he wanted to go.

Spinning around in the front seat his driver stared back at him shocked. "Are you sure about this, boss?"

"Yes, I'm sure you fucking dim-wit now turn you ass back around and take me there," Rex snapped resting his back against the smooth leather seats. Oh, he couldn't wait until he saw the surprise on their faces.

Chapter Sixteen

Lindow escorted Daria through the police station the same exact way he did the first time she was here. Hell, he would use any chance he got to touch her. He didn't like how his co-workers all stopped working and their eyes followed them until they reached his desk. It was like it was the first time that they had laid eyes on the pint size stunner in front of him. Sure, sometimes at home he stopped in his tracks to stare at her, but that didn't mean he wanted his co-workers doing the same thing.

"I wondered when you would decide to join us," A.J. complained, coming around the corner with a cup of coffee in his hand. He raked his eyes over Daria before he sat down at his desk.

"Don't start with that!" Lindow snapped pulling out his chair so Daria could sit down. "Can't you show some empathy for Ms. Jacobs? Her cousin might be dead."

A.J. took a couple of sips of his coffee before he sat the cup down on his desk. "Sorry, I don't have that for people that hide criminals from the law. We both know that she probably went to meet her cousin that night."

Lindow didn't miss how Daria avoided looking at either one of them.

"We don't know that for sure."

"If she hadn't keep Ronnie's whereabouts a secret maybe we wouldn't be wondering if that's his body or not," A.J. continued ignoring his comment.

"My cousin isn't dead," Daria hissed breaking into the conversation. "You don't know for sure if that's his body or not. I know you hate me, but that still doesn't mean you have the right to speak to me like this."

"You're right. I don't like you. I think the only reason Lindow is still sniffing around you is because you hadn't giving him a taste of you yet," A.J. replied snidely, lowering his voice so the entire station didn't hear them.

"You bastard," Lindow growled lunging for his partner of the past seven years, but Daria stuck out her hand and stopped him.

"Stop. I can handle this," Daria said. "How dare you say something like that with me sitting right here? Who in the hell do you think you are?"

"I'm the guy who's looking past the nice breasts and ass that my partner wants so bad," A.J. snarled no longer caring if everyone in the station heard him. "I won't let your looks blind me to the fact you could be working with your cousin."

"You better watch how you talk about me, Detective or I'll forget you're an officer of the court and hit the hell out of you," Daria warned.

"You do and I'll toss your ass in jail so fast that you'll forget your own name," A.J. tossed back.

Lindow was tired of this. He had to make his partner understand where this situation was going and the sooner the better. "A.J., you better stop before you say something that will get your further on my bad side," he snapped.

"Are you really going to take her side over mine? Damn man, we have been friends for years. Do you know how many cases we have worked together? Did you forget how many times I saved your ass out there?"

"This has nothing to do with our past. We need to work together to solve this case and you keep allowing your personal feelings to get in the way of it," Lindow said. "For once, can you not have the last word and work with us on this?"

A.J. glowered at him like he wanted to keep it going, but instead he nodded and then looked at Daria. "Ms Jacobs, I apologize for my early comments. They were uncalled for and out of line. I shouldn't have let my anger get the better of me."

Daria looked at Lindow, then back at A.J. like she didn't quite trust him. "How about we deal with each other and after this stay out of each other's way?" Her voice was loud and clear so he would get the message.

"Fine, I can agree to that." A.J. tersely agreed

Daria tossed A.J. a skeptical look as if she was trying to read his partner's thoughts. A part of Lindow wondered what A.J. was up to also, because he gave in a little too easily to his demands.

"Good, I'm glad that is settled because I need all my senses to deal with this, if is Ronnie," she exhaled.

"Do you think you're ready to view the body now?" A.J. asked taking a look at him over Daria's shoulder. His partner still looked pissed beyond belief at him and it was scaring him a little.

Daria said something under her breath that he couldn't understand then nodded. "I guess I'm ready as I'll ever be."

Standing up, A.J. gestured with his left hand towards a door at the far end of the hall way. "The coroner was given specific instructions not to start the autopsy on the body until you got a chance to see it. Right this way, Ms Jacobs."

Daria got out of her seat and looked at him. "Can I do this? What if it is really Ronnie? This will kill my dad. He told me to always take care of my cousin and I might have failed." She gave him a sad smile and then followed behind A.J.

"Wait," Lindow's deep voice rung out making Daria stop in her tracks.

"Yes?" Daria muttered turning back around. She looked so worried that it almost brought him to his knees. He couldn't let her do this alone.

"Do you want me to go with you instead of A.J.?" Lindow asked worried that his partner wouldn't give her enough compassion. Ronnie could actually be dead and he didn't think Daria was ready to realize that yet.

"No...I can go with A.J. to view the body. I rather have you here waiting for me when I get back." Daria gave him another small smile then turned and followed A.J. to where they had the body waiting for her.

Lindow stood back and watched the woman he was trying hard not to fall in love with leave with a man that hated the sight of her. He tried not to be hurt that she didn't want him there, but he understood too. She didn't want him to see her break down if it was Ronnie.

The urge to follow them made him take a couple of steps, then he stopped. No, he wouldn't do that. If Daria wanted to do this on her own then he would let her do it. Anyway he needed to talk to Captain Bell about something that has been on his mind for a while. Turning around and made his way back to his captain's office. Standing in front of door he knocked on the door once and waited.

"Enter," Captain Bell yelled over the ringing of the phones behind him.

Lindow opened the door and closed it quickly behind him so none of the air conditioning would leave the room. Captain Bell hated to be hot and always had his office set to a cooler temperature than the rest of the station.

"Sit down, Woods and tell me what brings you to my office," Captain Bell said taking a sip of his black coffee.

Sitting down in the chair in front of his boss' desk, Lindow stretched his legs out in front of them and crossed the at the ankle.

"You haven't heard about the problems A.J. and I are having now?' Lindow inquired, jumping right into the subject. Why would be beat around the brush? He wasn't getting along with A.J. anymore and everyone knew it.

Placing his cup back on the coaster Captain Bell raised one bushy eyebrow. "I thought that was just locker room talk. So, it's true about the tension between the two of you involving the Jacobs' woman?"

Lindow didn't like how his boss referred to Daria but he let it go. "Yes, A.J. and I aren't seeing eye to eye like we used to. He has a very bad opinion of my house guest and I don't like it."

"Is this Detective Woods talking or a boyfriend defending his girlfriend?" Captain Bell asked him. "You know better than to get involved with her."

"Daria isn't involved with me," he replied quickly. It wasn't like he wasn't trying though, but his little spitfire had an iron willpower when it came to him.

"I don't know if I believe you or not, especially after what A.J. told me."

"What did he open his big mouth and say to you?' Lindow asked. He was getting fed up with his partner more and more with each passing day.

"That the night he came over to watch her. She came into the room with her clothes hanging off her and you had a guilty look on your face," Captain Bell told him.

Son of a bitch! Lindow thought as the night flashed before his face. He knew A.J. wouldn't be able to keep his mouth shut. "It wasn't like that. Daria was headed towards her bedroom at the same time I opened the door for A.J."

Captain Bell just looked at him a few minutes without saying a word. "If that story didn't fly with your partner, why did you think it would with me?"

"I don't know," he shrugged. "But I can tell you that I'm not sleeping with Daria."

"Listen Woods, I've always thought of you like a son, but you can't let yourself fall for Ms. Jacobs. It will only hurt the case when it goes to trial. I don't care what you do after we arrest Rex for murder. But you can't let people think you are sleeping with our star witness' cousin."

"I told you I'm not sleeping with Daria," Lindow reiterated forcefully. *Yet*.

"Good....glad to hear it just make sure it doesn't happen. Remember your job comes first, not pleasing the head below your waist," Captain Bell informed him. "You have been on the force way too long to lose your job now."

Lindow didn't like how Captain Bell was more on A.J.'s side than his. "Are you saying I can't request another partner?"

"No....but I'll do this for you. I'll let A.J. do more of the legwork, talking to people about Ronnie and you can come in after he leaves for the day."

Lindow didn't think that was a bad deal, but he wasn't fond of leaving Daria at the house by herself at night. He still wasn't positive that she wouldn't make another run to talk to Ronnie again without him.

"I don't have all day. Is that a yes or no, detective?"

"Yes, I would like to do that." Lindow shook Captain Bell's hand and then left to go and wait for Daria.

It seemed like Daria and A.J. were gone for hours before they finally came back to the station, but Lindow was sitting at his desk waiting when they did. He couldn't tell by the look on Daria's face if it was her cousin or not. Instead of running to her like he wanted he kept his seat and let her come to him.

"Was it Ronnie?" Lindow asked the second Daria sat down in front of him.

"No... it was Ja'coby King, and someone beat him up so bad," she whispered brushing away tears from her eyes. "If they did that to him and he wasn't Ronnie, what would they do to my cousin if they find him?"

"They aren't going to do anything to Ronnie because we are going to find him first."

"Are you sure?" Daria asked.

"I promise you that I won't let anything happen to you cousin," Lindow swore secretly wishing and hoping that he'll be able to keep his word to her.

Chapter Seventeen

Daria sat in the tub with her back towards the closed bathroom door and shut her eyes. She couldn't believe the day she had. A.J. called and had Lindow bring her down to the police station to identify a body that wasn't even Ronnie's, but her heart went out to Ja'coby's family. She had to turn her head away after seeing it wasn't her baby cousin lying on that table. Whoever beat up Ja'coby made sure the poor boy would have a closed casket service.

Sinking deeper into the water, she let the warmth wash over her body and relaxed the tension in her neck and shoulders. It was getting harder and harder for her to fight off Lindow's advances. Today when he wrapped her up in his arms outside the station she almost lost her mind and kissed him. What in the world was wrong with her? She didn't date cops; let along kiss them by her own free will.

"I knew your body would be perfect," Lindow's rich masculine voice muttered behind her.

Shocked she glanced over her shoulder and found the object of her nightly dreams standing over her. Lindow had a clear vision of her body not covered up the bubbles. Had she been so lost in her own thoughts that she didn't even hear him come into the bathroom?

"What are you doing?" she asked trying to reach for a towel, but Lindow beat her to it and tossed it on the sink behind him.

"Looking at a very sexy, wet woman in my bathtub," he informed her dropping to his knees beside the bath tub.

"Well stop looking and move so I can get out of the tub," Daria exclaimed, hoping Lindow wouldn't pick up on how badly she wanted him to touch her.

"No, I can't do that because this is number four on my Daria-to-do list," Lindow whispered brushing a kiss at the back of her exposed neck.

She jerked at the feel of those well-formed lips at the base of her neck. Hell, she never realized how sensitive her skin was back there. Damn Lindow for finding that out. "I have already told you I don't care about that list."

A deep chuckle sent shivers over her wet skin. "Yes, you do my little spitfire. I wouldn't keep adding things to it them if I really thought you hated it."

Daria wanted to disagree but she couldn't. "Fine, what's the next item on that darn list?" she blurted out, unaware of the excitement in her voice.

"Number four on my list is I want to make you come apart in my tub," Lindow replied in a thick unsteady voice.

"Come...?" Daria started to ask, but the words got caught in her mouth as two of his fingers slid their way into her wet body.

Moaning she closed her eyes as her head fell back onto Lindow's hard chest. She shouldn't be letting him to this to her, Daria thought as Lindow added another finger. The sound of the water slapping against her body and his hand echoed in the quiet bathroom.

Using his free hand, Lindow spread her thighs a little wider then thrust his fingers deeper inside of her. "Do you know how much I would rather this be my cock that's aching inside of my pants now?" he breathed by her ear before he removed the hand on her thigh up to her breast.

Cupping her breast with Lindow tested its weight before he let it go and ran a calloused thumb over the left nipple making it even harder. "Baby, you're so tight. Do you know how I can't wait until I get a chance to feel you wrapped around me?"

She shook her head and tried to regain what common sense that she had left. "It's not going to happen," Daria purred as he sped up the pace of his fingers. She didn't know how much longer she could handle this.

"You're lying to yourself my little spitfire," Lindow murmured by her ear, stopping the movements of his fingers as his other hand still worked at her breasts. "Your body is burning up for me just as mine is for yours."

"No, it isn't," she denied trying to move her hips to find what she needed. She was so close again and Lindow was playing with her.

"Admit it," he whispered while his thumb brushing at the skin below her navel.

Daria bit down on her lip, so he couldn't hear her moans. She didn't want to let him know how right he was, but anymore of this damn torture and she do anything he wanted.

"Admit it," he demanded softly as he started working his fingers in and out of her body at a slower pace. "I can tell how close you are. This must be killing you," Lindow taunted by stopping his fingers again.

The hot throb of her body pushed any amount of common sense she had left right out of the window. "God, yes I want you. I want to make love to you so bad that I lay in my bed alone at night and fantasize about it," Daria screamed.

"Very good, my little spitfire," Lindow encouraged by her ear as he thrust his fingers deep in her body and gave her the release she needed.

“Oh, my God,” Daria moaned as she came back down. “I can’t believe that just happened. I don’t have enough energy to even get out of this tub.”

“I’ll take care of that, sweetheart,” Lindow breathed by her ear.

Picking Daria up out of the water, Lindow pressed her wet body to his and carried her out of the bathroom. He couldn’t believe how responsive this little minx was. Shit, he hadn’t meant to go that far with her.

He only wanted to tease her so she would finally admit her attraction to him. Hell, her warm, tight little body almost burnt his fingers off. If she hadn’t come when she did, he would have.

How could someone like Daria not belong to another guy? Well, he wasn’t going to be stupid and not stake his claim on her. She was already half his anyway. Her body had bloomed under his touch tonight, and those other times he went caressed that silky smooth skin of hers too. The only part to win over was her heart. As much as she wanted to deny it, Daria’s head was already into him. She just had to finally see it for herself first and the rest would be history.

Lindow looked at the soft bundle in his arms. He couldn’t stop the love that filled his heart. He hadn’t dreamt this pint size minx would be the woman he wanted to take care of for the next fifty years. Now all he had to do was make Daria realize it wouldn’t be so bad to love him back.

Could he get her to love him enough that she would leave that high positioned job in Washington, D.C. and move in with him? Did he make enough to offer the life that she had there? He might have to take baby steps with Daria, but he wasn’t about to let her go. He did have a pair of handcuffs by his bed for a reason.

Easing into her bedroom, he placed Daria on the bed and quickly covered her up with a cream colored sheet.

“Aren’t you going to stay here with me?” she asked, wrapping the sheet around her breast.

“Baby, I can’t. I’m already late and the captain isn’t going to be happy. I only stopped by the bathroom to tell you I was going to leave, but the sight you in the tub stopped me.”

“Can I do something to make you start here?” Daria dropped the sheet from around her waist.

Lindow sucked in a breath as his cock grew harder in his pants. Fuck, he had never been this hard in his life. Reaching down, he rubbed his hand over his erection hoping to ease some of the ache. It was hard enough for him carrying her from the bathroom to her own room instead of his.

But if he stayed in here a minute longer the added addition of her warm sweet-smelling bed would tempt his sanity and something might happen neither of them were quite ready for.

Bending down he brushed a kiss across her soft cheek and pulled the sheet back up. “Stop trying to entice me. I can’t stay.” He turned and hurried out of the room before he changed his mind.

Chapter Eighteen

Wandering around the room in her socks with a cup of hot tea in her hands, Daria looked at the note again that Lindow left taped to the bathroom door. Why did he always feel the need to tell her what to do? God, he was worse than her brothers.

I'll be at work most of the day. Do not leave the house for any reason and that does include looking for you cousin. Il soggiorno liberal'amore.

Lindow

Folding the note up Daria slid it in the front pocket of her black slacks and took another sip of her tea. She loved the little words of Italian that Lindow tossed at her every once in a while, but he never told her what any of it meant. The last time she asked about it his face closed up and she didn't bring it back up. Why would he hide something like that? She would never let him know it, but she thought it was so sexy when a man could speak another language.

Going back into the kitchen, she washed out the cup and placed it inside the dishwasher. Closing it she rested her back against it and stared out the window at the huge backyard that Lindow never seemed interested in. It looked so peaceful with the roses lined up around the back fence and the white bench tucked underneath an apple tree. All these things didn't resemble a bachelor pad this house seemed more for a couple with children. How did Lindow end up with a place like this?

Daria jumped when a loud knock pounded on the back door. She was more than a little nervous to open it. Who in the world would come to the back door instead of the front door? From the position she was standing in the person outside couldn't see her inside the house. Maybe if she stayed quiet they would just go away and leave her alone. She still hadn't fully recovered from the mind-blowing orgasm that Lindow gave her.

"Daria open the door," Ace yelled through the closed door. "Lindow sent me over here to check on you."

"What?" She stalked over to the door and flung it open. Ace didn't wait for her to invite him in instead he brushed his six foot frame past her and came right on in. "Don't wait for me to say come in," she muttered closing the door.

"I don't need a baby sitter." Daria couldn't help but noticed how attractive Ace was with his dark brown hair and royal blue eyes, but he didn't compare to his brother.

"Lindow told me you would say that." Ace chuckled taking a seat at the kitchen table. "He told you might try another disappearing act on him."

She pulled out a chair and joined Ace at the table. "How's your shoulder?"

Ace rotated his shoulder a couple of times then gave her a heart stopping grin that made a dimple pop out in his left cheek. "It's fine now. Sorry that I yelled at you that day. It had been a rough day at work."

"Don't worry about it," Daria said with a wave of her head. "You know that you don't have to stay here with me. I'm not going anywhere."

Ace grinned at her again and shook his head. "Lindow said you would try to pull that 'little miss innocent' routine too." He stretched his legs out in front of him and crossed his fingers over his flat stomach. She wondered how much women faked an emergency just to have Ace come to their houses.

"So, I guess that means you aren't leaving until Lindow comes back home?" Daria sighed already knowing the answer.

"You guessed right brown eyes," Ace answered with a wink.

"How about we get a cup of coffee at that coffee house around the corner? Just like old times?"

Lindow tossed the list of suspects down on his cluttered desk and stared at his partner with disbelief. Did A.J. really think he wanted to spend any time with him outside the station now? It was hard enough being civil inside the building with him. A.J. hated the woman he was falling in love with. A day never went by that a nasty resort hadn't come from his lips about Daria.

"No, I need to go over this list before I leave for the night," Lindow answered glancing back down at the paper. He didn't have the time or energy to get into it with A.J. tonight.

"I heard you on the phone talking to your brother," A.J. commented sitting down at his desk across from him.

"So?"

"Do you really trust Ace with Daria or vice versa?" A.J. asked. "If I remember correctly he did sleep with one of your girlfriends before. You know how a woman loves a man in uniform."

Lindow felt the tick in his jaw, but he swallowed down what his comment when Captain Bell ambled past his desk and went into his office. The second the door shut he gave A.J. a piece of him mind.

"First, Ace never had a clue I had been dating Sarah Michelle because he wasn't living here then. Secondly, Daria isn't like that. She wouldn't be involved with one man and sleeping with another one."

"If you say so," A.J. muttered. "But Ms. Jacobs is an attractive woman and your brother always had a weakness for a beauty."

Dropping his head into his hands Lindow slowly counted to ten and tried to dislodge the images of Daria and Ace together. Shit! Why was he listening to A.J. about Daria's behavior?

"I can tell you want to leave right now," A.J. whispered at him across their desks. "I know you want Daria, but don't let her pull the wool over your eyes. She isn't all miss sugar and spice. That woman is a temptress and you don't know how to break away from her."

God, what was A.J.'s deal with Daria? Why was he constantly picking on her or saying something bad about her? He had ran ideas over and over in his head, but none of would help his plan.

"Why don't you like Daria?" He just had to know.

"Daria is a little too high maintenance for me," A.J. complained. "She thinks all she has to do is wave a finger and the men will come running."

He didn't know where A.J. was getting this from. Daria wasn't any of those things. She was loving, caring, giving to a fault and had the biggest heart. No, he wasn't going to believe that was the real reason A.J. hated Daria.

"For some reason I don't believe you about Daria. There's another reason you hate her and I'll find out what it is." Leaning back in his chair, Lindow propped his feet on the end of his desk and stared at his partner. "Okay...it's time for you to tell me the truth."

Lindow opened the door to the sound of masculine laughter mingled in with feminine laughter coming for the game room at the very end of the hallway. Tossing his keys on the couch he made his way down toward the door, but stopped dead in his tracks when Daria sweet voice whispered. "You know that's too big for you to stick right there."

"Hey, you never know unless you let me try, so open your legs a little wider so I can shove it in there. I can promise you it wouldn't hurt."

He felt like his world was crumbling at his feet as he inched closer to the door and waited for Daria's response. "You told me that earlier and I was in a lot of pain after we finish that time."

Hell, this was one time that Ace wasn't going to get what he wanted, Lindow thought as he stormed the rest of the way down the hallway. Turning the doorknob, he flung open the door and rushed into the room. The sight in front of him stopped him from speaking one word.

Ace had one of his hands between Daria's legs while the other one was dangling over her left breast. Daria had her positioned between's Ace's with her head turned at an odd angle. "Hey bro. Why don't you come in here a join us?" Ace yelled placing his dangling hand on the red circle on the floor.

Daria glanced at him from the corner of her eye and smiled. "Yeah join us so I can beat another Woods man at the game of Twister." She grinned placing her hand on the yellow circle on the other side of his brother's leg.

Lindow shut the door and calmed down the anger that was still simmering in his body. He had been trying for weeks to get Daria wrapped around his body like that and his brother does in a matter of hours.

"How did the two of you end up playing Twister at this time of night?" he questioned noticing how Ace's was staring at Daria's tight butt in her snug jeans. The memory of what A.J. said popped into his mind. "Hey, how about you stop playing that and we play another game I can join in?"

Ace glanced up at him with a frown before he quickly unwrapped his body from around Daria and stood up. "This game isn't over brown eyes. I want a rematch."

Daria sat down on the Twister mat and brushed the hair from her eyes then smiled at his brother. "Get off of it. You know that you can't beat me. You just used your brother as an excuse to stop playing the game. I had you down and out twenty minutes ago."

Lindow wasn't pleased with the way Daria was kidding along with Ace. She never smiled at him like that or teased him. She always found a way to push him away. Folding his arms across his chest, he cleared his throat a couple of times. Ace and Daria's heads swung in his direction. "Thanks for staying here with Daria, but its okay for you to leave now. I don't want to keep you from anything, Ace."

"Um.....yeah sure there is a card game at the station today that I wanted in on," Ace replied. He picked his jacket up off the half sofa and headed toward the door. "I'll hold you to that rematch, Daria," he grinned before going out the door.

Lindow's emerald gaze narrowed at the sexy woman sitting on the floor staring up at him. He was still feeling the sting of jealousy at how friendly she was being with his brother. Did she have a thing for firefighters and not cops?

"Hey are you going to stand there and glare at me all night?" Daria asked. "Or are you going to help me up off this floor?" She stuck out her small hand and waited for him.

Sighing, he moved over to the end of the Twister mat and wrapped his hand around Daria's. But instead of pulling her up she tugged him down causing him to land on his side. Lindow quickly rolled over to his back and the same time Daria crawled on his chest.

"I missed you while you were at work." She breathed by his lips kissing the corner.

Yeah right. "I don't know if I should believe you or not." he pouted running his hands up and down her back dragging the pink t-shirt, so he could touch her bare back. "You seemed awful comfortable rolling around on the floor with Ace," Lindow complained jealously.

Laughing, Daria placed her hands on the either side of his head and brought her face down until they were nose to nose. "I'm only going to say this once, so listen very closely...my sexy detective."

His heart missed at beat at the soft purring sound of Daria's voice. He didn't know what to say, so he just continued to stare up into her dark eyes. He wasn't use to this side of Daria. He wasn't going to make a move until he heard her out. "I'm listening my little spitfire."

"I don't want your brother," she told him. "I saw the look on your face when you stormed into the room. How could you think I would want another man after the pleasure you gave me last night?"

Lindow glanced away before he looked at the breathtaking woman lying on top of him. "How did I know that you didn't have a soft spot for firefighters?" He worked his hands further under Daria's shirt and unsnapped her bra.

"No....sorry I don't have a soft spot for that particular Woods man, but I do know one that can get me hot and bothered the second he saunters into a room," Daria told him, working at the buttons on his shirt.

Lindow captured Daria's hand between his two larger ones. "Daria we have to stop," he moaned under his breath, cursing Daria's timing and his bad luck. "We can't make love....yet." He added they "yet" so she would know that it was in their near future.

Daria jerked her hand away from his and jumped off the Twister mat to stand above him. "Why can't we? Are you saying that your penis is too good to put in me?" she hissed at him before she turned to leave the room.

Jumping up off the slippery mat Lindow caught Daria before she stormed out the door. He wrapped his arms around her struggling body and jerked her back against his chest. "My little spitfire I've been thinking of ways to get my cock inside of the hot tight little body of yours for a while now."

"Stop lying," Daria hissed pulling at his hands. "You don't want me, so why lie about it."

Twirling her around his arms, he grabbed of one Daria's hands and pressed it against the front of his tented slacks. "If I don't want you then what in the hell is this?" he growled making her cup his throbbing erection in the palm of her small hand.

"A reaction," she retorted brushing her fingers across him.

He bit back a moan and controlled the movement of hips so he wouldn't buck against her palm. "You know damn well it's more than that," he told her removing Daria's sweet touch before he did something stupid.

"Fine if you really want to have sex with me....then why did you stop?" Daria questioned with a confused look on her face.

"Sex...oh my little spitfire...I want more than that from you and for us." Lindow shook his head and tugged an unwillingly Daria back in his arms. "I don't want to have sex with you...I want us to make love until neither one of us can move."

"So, what's stopping you?"

"Condoms," he muttered kissing the side of her mouth.

"What?" Daria moaned pressing her chest against his.

He could still feel the hard imprint of her nipples through her thin shirt. It was killing him not to act on it. "I don't have any condoms in the house unless you're willingly to let me love you without one. This little seduction of yours has to wait until tomorrow night." God, why didn't he buy some damn condoms after the first night she stayed over? He couldn't believe how his stupid mistake was coming back to haunt him now.

Daria opened his shirt and ran her nails over his chest. "I don't know how I feel about giving you a rain check on this ," she teased. "I might not feel in the mood tomorrow night."

Oh...you'll be in the mood even if I have to pull another item off my Daria-to-do list to make you agree to my request, Lindow thought as he pulled Daria hands from his shirt. "I don't have a doubt that this flame will still be burning bright tomorrow night."

"How can you be so sure I'll want you tomorrow?" Daria questioned.

"Because of this..." Lindow hissed before he jerked his favorite little attorney back into his arms for a tongue dueling kiss. He didn't know long the kiss lasted, but when it ended Daria was pressed against his chest gasping for breath.

"Damn I hate when you're right," she breathed against his shirt.

"I usually do too my little spitfire, but tonight isn't one of those nights," he exclaimed before he swept Daria under in arms.

Daria laid her head on his shoulder and looked up into his eyes. "What are you doing? I thought you didn't want to have sex....sorry make love," she corrected after he gave her a hard glare.

"I do want you make love. We just can't at the moment, but I can still get pleasure from just holding you in my arms and watching you fall to sleep," he exclaimed placing a kiss on her forehead as he carried Daria out of the game room for his bedroom.

Lindow didn't want to think about the future and what would happen once Ronnie was found, but one thing was clear in his mind-Daria Jacobs wasn't going to leave him. It didn't matter how hard she fought him, she was staying right here with him for the rest of his life.

Chapter Nineteen

"Please tell me that you have good news for me," Rex stuck the end of his cigar inside his mouth and sucked on the tip. He never smoked the damn things he just liked how they tasted in his mouth. Plus, it gave him the harder look he liked to portray to his boys.

"Sorry, Mr. Staples, but she hasn't left the house in days," Gary said standing in front of his desk. "Plus, she is never alone inside the house now. We were going to make a surprise visit yesterday until that Detective's brother showed up and he didn't leave until Woods came home."

He hated when he plans didn't work when he wanted them too. Daria was one tasty looking woman from a distance, but he still hadn't the pleasure of speaking to her up close and personal. Women like her made his cock harden in his pants just from one glimpse.

No wonder Gary wanted a taste of that bitch; she looked like one good ride. He would bet his entire drug ring that Detective Woods went to bed and woke up every morning a very happy man. There was no way he wasn't hitting that tight ass living under his roof.

"Well, we have to think of a way to get Ms. Jacobs out in the open," he exclaimed tossing the cigar into the ash tray by his elbow. "I think it's about time that we had some face time with her. Don't you Gary?"

Gary's tongue darted out and he licked his lips. "I sure do boss," he grinned, rubbing his hands together. "Can I have face time with her first? I still owe her for what she did to me."

Standing up, Rex fixed his two thousand dollar suit and glanced at his reflection at the mirror on his desk. "It all depends on how you get Ms. Jacobs out of Detective Woods' house and in my presence. If you do that without messing up, than I might let you play a little hide and go seek with that luscious body of hers."

Gary flashed him a smile showing off his new gold tooth that he just purchase last week with extra money he gave him.

"Nice tooth," Rex stated.

"Thanks, I like it too. That extra money you gave me for getting rid of Ja'coby really came in handy," Gary grinned. "It was too bad that Marcus was out of town on family business and wasn't able to get his cut."

"It was such a shame that his sister got attacked while walking back from the campus library. Who would do such a thing like that?" Rex asked, coming around his desk to stare at Gary.

Swallowing hard, Gary quickly took a step back from him. "I always told Marcus with a sister that sexy, she was bound to draw some unwanted attention. I just hope he doesn't get any crazy ideas in his head."

"I don't think Marcus will get any kind of thoughts in his head because he wouldn't want his sister to get a repeat performance," Rex replied heading for the door. "By the way, Gary you have twenty four hours to bring Ms. Jacobs to me." The last sound Rex left Gary with was the door closing behind him.

"Can I trust you to stay inside this home while I go and check out a lead on Ronnie?" Lindow asked fixing his gun holster over his shoulder. Last night he had woken up with Daria curled up next to him and everything had felt right in the world. He didn't know how he was going to make it today at work. All day long his mind was going to be thinking about that box of condoms he had to buy. Not even A.J. was going to put a damper on the day for him. He was just glad this wasn't one of the nights he had to work late, because he didn't think he'd make it.

"Yes. You can trust me to stay in the house." Daria agreed glancing away from him. "However, I'm tired of staying locked up in this house all the time. Ronnie is my family and I want to help find him. Have you completely forgotten that I'm a lawyer? I'm used to dealing with criminals in Washington, D.C.," Daria tossed in with a fire in her eyes. She was going to tell Lindow soon about Ronnie because she was beginning to hate lying to him. But she had wanted to find out who Ronnie was so scared of first.

"Let me go with you. I can help you talk to people about Ronnie. You know most black males don't trust law enforcement as it is."

Lindow hated to admit that Daria did have a point. Half the black youths in this city wouldn't talk to A.J. once they found out he was a cop. But he didn't want to put Daria in harms way. She was so focused on finding Ronnie that she never paid any attention to the things going on around her.

"If you let you come with me and talk to certain people, do you promise not to go overboard with the questions?" he asked watching the happiness radiate from her gorgeous face.

“I promise I won’t go overboard with the questions,” Daria agreed rushing away from his to pick up her purse off the couch. “Let’s go,” she yelled brushing past him heading for the door.

He hoped he hadn’t made a mistake by allowing her to come with him. Lindow knew that Daria had made him that promise but he didn’t believe she had the capability of keeping it. Snatching the keys off the table, he followed Daria to the door and hoped the day would go better than he thought it would.

On the way to the station all he could think about was how much the woman next to him had wrapped him entire body around her petite finger. He had never in the past thought about having sex with a woman without protection. However, last night shoving Daria away from him was the hardest thing he had ever done.

His eyes dropped to her flat stomach and his heart started to beat a little faster. The thought of Daria growing big with his child didn’t scare the hell out of him. Really it made him wanted to forget all about buying the condoms after work and seduce her into taking him without one.

The sound of Daria’s cell phone ringing drew him out of his daydream and he wondered who was calling his woman. He kept driving but listened in on her conversation.

“Hello?” Daria whispered.

“When are you planning on being back at work?” a gruff familiar voice yelled at her from the other end.

Daria rolled her eyes at the sound of Alison’s voice on the other side. “You know that I still have some vacation time that I haven’t used up,” she tossed back.

“I didn’t think you would still be on vacation,” Alison whined back at her. “I need you back here by the end of next month. If you aren’t don’t worry about coming back at all,” he threatened.

“You don’t have the power to fire me Alison,” she snapped. “Only one of the partners only has the power to do that.”

“See if you had been here you would have known that I made senior partner yesterday,” Alison snickered.

Daria felt her heart down to the bottom of her stomach. "How in the hell is that possible? You haven't made partner. All the cases you won in the past were because of my help." She hissed.

"Yeah....thanks for the assistance because that Newman cause you helped me research gave me the extra points I needed in their eyes," Alison gloated. "See...I knew you were more that a tight piece of ass in a short skirt. There's actually a pretty good brain in that heads of yours."

She blinked back the tears burning the back of her eyes. Alison knew she was up for that job and he stole it from her. How could she go back home and work for a bastard like him? She would never get anywhere now with him over her.

"You can't talk to me like that," Daria exclaimed. "I can file sexual harassment charges against you."

"Go right ahead," Alison taunted. "I'll just say you got upset I called you and told you to come back to work. With the way you missed all those days a few months ago, I have a good case against you too. You aren't keeping your part of the contract you signed."

She hated that Alison was right. "Fine, I'll remember what you told me."

"You better," Alison uttered than the phone went dead.

Snapping the phone lid back down, Daria tossed it back into her purse and wiped the tears away from her eyes. She worked too hard for that bastard to talk to her like that. She didn't need his arrogant attitude reprimanding her along with everything she had going on with Ronnie.

Hell, she'll be back in Washington, D.C. in a month, but only if all of this mess was over with Ronnie. She wasn't about to let Alison tell her how to live her life outside that high rise office.

"Who in the hell was that on the phone?"

Closing her eyes Daria groaned and turned her head toward the window. How could she forget about Lindow? "It was no one."

"Don't lie to me."

She didn't have time for Lindow to get all protective on her. She needed her mind clear to think about how she was going to handle her future. "I'm not lying to you."

Lindow left her alone and kept driving until they pulled into the parking lot of the police station. She reached over to open the car door, but Lindow's hand shot out and stopped her. "Tell me who was on the phone. I don't like seeing you upset like this."

Dropping her hand she spun around and found Detective Woods face directly in hers. "It doesn't involve you or anything about this case. Why would I tell you about it?"

She didn't miss the hurt look at passed across Lindow's handsome features and instantly regretted her words. Daria reached out and touched Lindow's shirt when he started to move away from her. "Wait...I'm sorry. It's just that Alison has that effect on me. After I talk to him I'm always in a bad mood."

"Alison...is a guy?" Lindow asked. "Who is he to you?"

Daria noticed the jealous tone of Lindow's voice and laughed. If she and Alison were the two last people on the planet and had to reproduce the human race would die. "Alison is my boss. He told me that if I wasn't back at work by the end of next month that I would no longer have a job." She purposely left out the rest of the conversation.

A long finger stroking the side of her jaw drew her wavering attention back to Lindow. "Tell me the rest."

She opened her mouth to lie and then shut it when she realized it wouldn't do any good. Lindow knew her too well now. "Alison stole the job I wanted. He won less high profiled cases, but he still got made partner," Daria snapped. "I know his father had something to do with it, but I won't be able to prove it."

"Do you think you coming here looking for Ronnie was the real reason you got passed over for the job?"

" I think that could been a part of it. Plus me being an intelligent black woman didn't help my case any. No...my job is a boy's club kind of place. If you're a man you get the better opportunities."

"I thought those kinds of places didn't exist anymore," Lindow said running his thumb across the bottom of her ear. "Can't they get in trouble for doing that to you?"

Daria shivered at Lindow's light touch. He knew what he was doing to her, but she wasn't about to make out with him in front of the police station. "Alison is smart. I'll give that to him. He knew what he was doing. So, I'll have a hard time proving my case against him. His father retired for the firm six months ago and was grooming Alison to take make partner. I just didn't think it would happen this fast." She grabbed his hand and removed it away from her face. "I can't think about that now."She reached for the door again only to have Lindow pull her back to him. "Fine... we can work on Ronnie all day, but tonight when we get back home you won't be thinking about anyone but me. I want your mind on me and how many orgasms your body can handle in one night." Lindow kissed her behind the ear and got out of the car.

Daria sat in the front seat her body humming from the words Lindow just breathed by her ear. Damn it to hell, that man knew how make a woman almost come without the need of penetration, she thought as Lindow opened her car door.

Chapter Twenty

I can't believe she's acting like I'm not even in the room. Lindow took a sip of his cold coffee grimaced and then placed it back down on the table. Daria had spent the past hour looking over mug shots with one of the rookie officers. She wasn't every twenty feet away from him, but she acted like he wasn't there. Not once during that entire time had she searched the room for him. He could have left and she would never known it.

He didn't want to feel the spark of jealously when Officer Collins touched her arm and pointed out a mug shot at the top of the other page. He knew she was here for a reason, but his ego was stinging a little. What if she had forgotten about their plan to make love tonight? Hell, he had even gotten up early and rushed out to buy two boxes of condoms while she slept.

Lindow almost snapped with disapproval and a slow burning jealousy worked its way through his body when he saw another officer hurry off and get Daria a cup of water. Hell, none of these guys ever paid this much attention to any other witness. But he had to admit Daria did look stunning in her white wraparound shirt and matching Capri pants. He almost made her go back and change when he laid his eyes on her this morning.

"Detective Woods if you have a minute could you come in my office," Captain Bell ordered.

He took one last long lingering look at Daria before he got up and went into his boss' office. "Yes, how can I help you, sir?"

"First, stop drooling over Ms. Jacobs and pretend to be earning the nearly nonsexist paycheck the state of Nevada gives you," Captain Bell complained. "You have been sitting their staring a hole into the side of her face. It's bothering me, so I can only dream what it is doing to her."

Lindow felt his face growing warm under Captain's Bell reprimand. "I apologize, sir. I can promise that it won't happen again." He didn't want to make Captain Bell to tell him that he wouldn't be able to bring Daria to the station anymore. He enjoyed having the light scent of her perfume around his desk and inside his car. She made his work environment more pleasurable and A.J. being assigned to footwork for this case only added to his relaxation.

"Good...you're an excellent detective when you focus is on your job. Now, I don't want to have this discussion with you again, Detective Woods."

Lindow had never felt so embarrassed in his life that his desire for Daria was so strong that even his boss could see it. "I swear, I'll keep it at home."

Captain Bell glanced at him over his glasses and nodded. "Now, I did call you in here for a reason other than the attractive Ms. Jacobs. I heard that Rex is planning to open up another drug warehouse."

"Meth or Crack?" Lindow asked, sitting up straighter in his seat. They both knew that half of Las Vegas was on drugs supplied by Rex Staples, but they still hadn't been able to locate anymore drug houses since Rex was released. It always seemed like when they got word of one, Rex had it burnt down to the ground before they could gather any evidence.

"I'm not sure, but I think it's going to be heroine," Captain Bell groaned taking off his glasses he flung them on his desk. "How much more power can this bastard get in this town?"

"Sir...I don't know...but we need to stop him before he gets this next place up and running," Lindow complained. He didn't want any more kid's deaths of his hands. It was bad enough one child had already died from Rex's poison.

"Don't blame yourself. We got to that poor boy too late. Rex knew he was giving that kid too much and he didn't care."

He didn't want to shoulder the blame, but he did. Rex had been his major case for the past two years and he was still a step behind the smug S.O.B. "I know, but I can't wait until the day I get to slap the cuffs on him."

"I know," Captain Bell agreed. "If we find Ronnie, his testimony could get Rex life behind bars. Has Daria giving you any kind of hint where her cousin might be at? Has he tried to contact her again?"

"No....I guess the last time she was with him, Daria gave him enough money to tie him over. I wouldn't even know about this if one of my snitches didn't tell me about it. Daria is clueless that I know she saw him the other night."

"She's trying to protect him because he's family, but that is going to hurt in him the end," Lindow complained. He didn't want to be hurt, but he was. Daria still didn't trust him.

"Ronnie is a crafty kid. He won't contact Daria unless he really needs her help, so I'm guessing he's about ready for another visit. Whatever you do be sure to follow Daria and find out where he is. That's the only reason I didn't have you arrest her when I found out she was hiding Ronnie from us."

He hated what he was doing to Daria, because he really did care about her. However, Captain Bell was right. Ronnie needed to be found and placed in protective custody. Rex couldn't get to Ronnie before they did or he'd end up like the boy that they pulled from the lake last week.

"You won't be disappointed, sir. I'm going to find Ronnie and bring him back to the station," Lindow promised getting up out of the seat.

"I hope that you do because that's the only way we can get Rex on murder charges," Captain Bell informed sliding his glasses back on his face door.

Lindow looked at his boss one time before he left and he knew that he was on a short lease when it came to his job. He didn't ever bother to glance at Daria as he went downstairs to the evidence room. He knew she was still sitting in the corner enjoying all the attention that the other officers were tossing her way.

Daria hurried down the steps one of the officers' pointed her to after she realized that Lindow was no longer sitting at his desk. She was here to help him find her cousin and he just abandoned her after he left his boss' office. What in the hell was wrong with him now? She didn't know how to read him anymore. He was in such a bad mood all the time now.

She walked down the long flight of steps until she reached the bottom. Walking around she looked around for Lindow but she didn't see him anywhere. Maybe the officer was wrong and Lindow didn't come down here after all. It was amazing to see all the things bagged and labeled placed on shelves along the walls.

She started back for the stairs until she realized there could be something down here that could help her case with Ronnie. Rushing back to the bottom step, Daria glanced up the steps and made sure that the guard was gone to get her a glass of water. She was still amazed she got him to leave the door unlocked for her after a few tears and complaining about stomach cramps.

Easing back from the steps, Daria went back to the shelves but she didn't know which one to search first since there were about ten of them in the room. Glancing around, she decided to look at the ones at the very back of the room by a door. It would give her more time to look through the bags.

As her hand reached for a green evidence bag in the middle of the shelf, a warm hand covered her mouth and a strong arm wrapped around her waist jerking her quickly into a side room.

Daria struggled against a hard warm body as fear rushed through her veins. She tried to get loose but her attacker pressed her body against the cool wall. As the hand was removed it was quickly replaced by a pair of warm firm lips that belonged to Lindow.

"You aren't supposed to be down here," Lindow breathed by the side of her mouth.

Sliding her arms around his strong neck she brushed her body over his. "I was looking for you," she moaned as his thick erection jerked against her stomach. "Your body doesn't act like it's too upset to see me."

"You know that he's always very happy to feel his favorite lady." Lindow groaned as he grabbed her hips. "Are you ready for tonight?" he asked, drawing the skin below her ear between his teeth.

Daria bit down on her bottom lip to keep from screaming out her frustration. God, how much longer was it before Lindow got off from work? She didn't know how much longer she could wait. "You aren't playing fair," she groaned. Lindow knew her body stayed at a slow burn for him and he was using that against her.

"You weren't playing fair earlier when you had all of my co-workers drooling over you," Lindow growled jerking her hips to his.

Grinning, Daria worked at the buttons on Lindow's shirt under they were completely undone. She pulled his shirt from his slacks then ran her fingernails through his chest hair. She liked how his big body shivered under her touch. Her fingers tunneled through the hair until they found one hard male nipple.

She kept brushing her thumb over it until Lindow dropped his head against the door and his cock jerked. "Hmmm....it seems like I found your weakness."

"My little spitfire....anytime you place that cute little hands anywhere on my body it goes weak for you," Lindow groaned.

"Hey....that's very good to know," she retorted as she continued to play with his nipple. Taking her free hand Daria unzipped Lindow's slacks and slid her hand inside. "It seems like that you don't like to wear underwear." Daria whispered running her thumb over the tip of his warm erection.

"Shit! What are you doing to me?" Lindow panted as he thrust his cock into the palm of her hand. "Do you know how much trouble I'll get into if the Captain find us doing this at the station. I'm an officer of the law and this could get me in a lot of trouble."

Standing on tiptoes she ran the tip of her tongue along the side of his jaw. "Here I thought you were the type that liked to live dangerously. Besides if I had to make a bet

I'm sure we aren't the first people to make out in a police station." She squeezed his hardened cock and slowly slid her hand down its growing length. "Maybe I was wrong and we should stop. I don't want you to take the risk and get fired."

"You want to see dangerous my little spitfire then I'll show you dangerous." Lindow growled removing her hand from his body.

Picking her up Lindow carried her across the room and laid her down on a cot. He took off his holster and laid it on a shelf next to them then took off his shirt tossing it on the floor. "You have been tempting me all day long in those tight Capri's and I am about to do something about it."

"Oh, I didn't think you noticed how cute I looked in my outfit." Daria teased rising up on her elbows.

"You knew I wanted to drag you back home to the bedroom and make love to you," Lindow snapped undoing his pants as he stared down at her. He pushed them down his hips and kicked them over near his shirt.

She didn't get time to enjoy the sexy man's body in front of her before he was taking off her clothes and tossing them on top of his. "You can't be serious about us having sex in the police station," Daria gasped as Lindow covered her body. "I was only teasing you."

"I haven't been more serious about anything in my life." He whispered licking her nipple. "Damn you taste so good," Lindow groaned. "Captain Bell had the cot brought down here for emergencies and this is definitely one of those."

Daria tried to think of something to make Lindow stop, but all thought left her mind when he slid two of his thick fingers into her body. Arching her back she made them penetrate her even further. "Oh...that feels so good," she panted.

"Hot little thing aren't you?" Lindow taunted working his fingers in and out of her body. "Do you still think we need to stop or do you want to see if we get caught?"

"I don't care anymore," she groaned. "I just don't want you to stop what you're doing to me. It can't get any better than this."

"My little beauty, I have to disagree with you," Lindow chuckled as he withdrew his wonderful fingers from her body. "Don't you move from this spot," he whispered licking her navel before he rolled off the body.

Daria tried to marshal her common sense for the few seconds that Lindow was gone away from her. She was a top notch lawyer. If it got out she was having sex in a police station basement her career would be over. But right at the moment, she didn't give a damn. She was tired of doing things for other people. This moment in time was for her. She felt the cot dip as Lindow positioned his body over hers.

"Do you know how many times I fantasized about making love to you after I first saw you in that courtroom?" He asked nibbling at the sides of her breasts. "Or how many different ways that I wanted to take this perfect body of yours?"

She trembled as Lindow slid her legs apart and slipped his huge body between them. The hair on his legs tickled the inside of her thighs. Reaching up Daria ran her nails down the muscles in Lindow's back.

"Warm...you're so warm."

"Only for you my love...only for you," he whispered, licking the side of her neck. "The scent of your body always gets my blood hot, sending it racing through my veins."

Daria trembled as Lindow's words raked over her sweat covered body. She was trying to be the stronger one, but she wanted him so bad that she would take it. "When do I get to feel some of that heat?" she asked stroking Lindow's lower back with her fingertips.

"You don't have to ask me twice," Lindow growled taking her with one sure thrust. They both hissed at the first touch of him inside her dripping body. It was like her body had been make for this and nothing was going to stop her from taking pleasure in every second.

Daria couldn't control the gasp of surprise that erupted from her. It felt so good to have a man inside of her body after two years. Lindow's cock throbbed in her body making her squirm on the bed.

"Oh...you feel so good," she whispered lifting up her hips to get him ever close.

"Stop...my little spitfire," Lindow groaned as he thrust in and out of her wet body. "You can't keep moving like that or it will be over before it starts. I've wanted you for months so let me enjoy it."

Grabbing her by the knees Lindow moved her legs further apart and increased his long sure strokes. "Do you know how hot you look beneath me?" he questioned leaning over to draw her nipple into his mouth.

She couldn't talk. How could she when Lindow was doing such delicious thing to her body? The sound of their slick bodies sliding over each other echoed in the cool room. There wasn't a part of her body that she didn't want touched by Lindow before the day was over.

Her body clenched around Lindow's thick warm erection even tighter when his mouth let go of her nipple and pinched it with his fingers. An erotic shot of lust shot through her, settling where she and the man giving her so much pleasure were connected.

"Shit...this is better than any wet dream I had about you months ago," his heated voice panted above her. "I don't want this to ever end." Lindow groaned placing his head beside her neck.

"Neither do I...lover," Daria hissed raising her hips to meet Lindow thrust for thrust. "It isn't enough." She complained trying to get her body closer to his but couldn't.

"I know. I need more, too," Lindow grunted as he flipped on his back pulling her on top of him.

He raised her over his long thick cock and thrust deep into her body sending tiny shock waves through her. She didn't know making love could feel this good. Over and over, Lindow brought her down over his length until her body jerked and released all the built up tension that had been building for months.

She fell to his solid warm chest exhausted as she felt him find her release beneath her. Brushing her hair back from her face, Lindow kissed her temple.

"Damn...honey you know how to wear an old man out."

"Well for an old man you sure know how to work that body of yours," she sighed snuggling closer to his damp body.

"Daria....I would love to stay with you like this," Lindow murmured running his hands down her back to cup her butt. "But we just made love in the police station basement. We need to get back upstairs and fast."

"OH MY GOD!" Daria screamed jumping off Lindow body. "I completely forgot about that." She rushed across the room and threw her clothes back on while Lindow got back into his."I bet everyone is wondering what happened to us. There's no telling what they're saying about us upstairs," she stated agitatedly hurrying toward the door.

A strong hand wrapped around her arm stopping her in mid-step. Spinning her back around Lindow placed a finger under her chin and made her look at him. "If I hear them say one derogatory word about you they'll regret it."

"You know that we have been gone awhile?" she tossed back jerking her chin and body away from his touch. If his hand stayed on her body any longer they would end up back in that bed less than twenty feet behind them.

"Daria....wait!" Lindow yelled after her, but she kept walking to the door. She opened it and went out without looking back.

Chapter Twenty One

"Hey, brown eyes where are you going?" Ace questioned at Daria flung over the opened the police station door. She almost knocked him over as she raced down the steps onto the sidewalk. He didn't have a clue what was going on, but he was about to find out.

"Daria....shit I told you to wait," Lindow screamed rushing out of the station right behind her.

"Lindow, what in the hell is going on?" Ace asked, grabbing his brother by the arm.

"Ace...let go of me. I can't let her be out here by herself like this. Marcus and Gary are still out there looking for her," Lindow growled snatching his arm away.

Ace looked at Daria who was almost at the end of the corner. "Okay....I don't know what is wrong between the two of you, but she doesn't want to talk to you. So, let me go after her and calm her down."

Lindow stared at him hard. "Will you take her back home and stay with her until I get off in a couple of hours?"

"Yeah...sure we can play another game of Twister," he teased.

"The hell you will. Just stay with her. I don't want your hands all over her. Do you understand me, Ace?" Lindow didn't have a problem beating his brother down in front of the station.

Ace turned and hurried down the steps toward his car. "Yeah, I understand," he yelled over his shoulder as he got inside his car. He took a quick glance in the rearview mirror and saw his brother go back inside the station. Pulling out of the parking space, he drove down the street and stopped in front of Daria as she tried to cross the street.

"Get in and I don't want you to tell me no," Ace yelled at Daria as he reached across the seat and pushed open the passenger side door.

Daria glowered at him, but she got into the car and slammed the door shut. He waited until she had fastened her seat belt before he drove off. From the corner of his eye, Ace looked at Daria and wondered how did his brother luck out and get someone as hot as her. She was not the kind of woman his brother usually went for.

"Want to tell me why you are running out of the police station away from my brother?" he asked turning the car left at the corner.

"Alec, I don't want to talk about it," she answered brushing her hair back from her face. "I just want to forget this day ever happened."

Sounded like something happened at the station, he thought. "Did you get some bad news about your cousin?"

Daria shook her head. "No, it was nothing like that. Ronnie is still in hiding and Woods is still trying to find him."

Woods? When did Daria stop calling his brother by his birth name? "So, it was something personal that happened between the two of you, wasn't it?" he questioned.

"Why would you say that?"

Ace took his left hand off the wheel and tapped the seam showing on Daria's shoulder from her shirt. "Well for one thing your shirt is on the wrong side and I'm can bet money you didn't leave the house that away."

She jerked away from him and glanced down at her shirt running her fingers across the exposed seams at the bottom. "I'm so embarrassed," Daria muttered pulling at her shirt.

He heard the pain in her voice and felt bad for pointing the shirt out to her. Stopping a gas station at the corner Ace pulled inside and parked inside an empty spot. "Hey it's nothing to be embarrassed about. My brother has that effect on women," Ace assured her, patting Daria on the shoulder. "Why don't you go to the bathroom and I'll wait for you here. It's right around the corner."

Touching him on the back of the hand, Daria smiled at him before she got out of the car and hurried around the corner. He couldn't take his eyes off how the Capri's hugged her tight butt. If his brother wasn't already in love with the enticing attorney, he would shake some sense into him until he was. Daria was the perfect woman for his temperamental brother.

Ace switched the radio on to his favorite station and relaxed in the car. He didn't think it should take Daria that long to fix her shirt and then maybe he could talk her into stopping for an ice cream cone before he took her home. Hell, what woman would turn down a scoop of double chocolate ice cream?

Checking her reflection for the last time in the mirror Daria turned on the faucet and splashed some cold water on her face. She still couldn't believe she had sex in the basement of the police station.

Have I lost my mind?

God, if Alison got wind of this back home she would be fired for sure. He was always looking for a way to get rid of her and now she just served him one on a silver platter.

She lost her mind the second Lindow's hands started caressing her body. Why didn't she have any willpower when it came to that man? Sure, it was one of the finest men she had ever laid eyes on, but to have sex with him in the police station wasn't her. All her co-workers at the law office wouldn't believe it if someone told them Little Miss Rules and Regulations stripped naked and had more than one earth shattering orgasms with a cop.

Turning off the water, she grabbed a couple of paper towels and wiped her hands off. Well, she wasn't going to let that happen again with Lindow.

"You can do this," Daria uttered talking to her reflection in the mirror. "Don't let Lindow's scent or rock hard body tempt you anymore." She tried to burn that into her mind and sent up a silent prayer that she could stay strong.

Daria unlocked the bathroom door and went back outside blinking a couple of times when the sunlight hit her in eye. She moved a few steps toward the corner of the building when a knife was press against her back and a rag covered in chloroform was placed over her nose and mouth. She tried to struggle until a raspy voice whispered in her ear.

"I don't have problem killing you after what you did to my ear." Gary hissed pressing the knife into the small of her back. "But my boss wants you alive."

Those were the last words she heard before the drug took over her body making her pass out.

"I don't see why I can't spend a few minutes alone with the bitch." The pissed off male's voice snapped. "I was the one who found her, like Rex wanted and brought her back here."

"Gary, hell you know the damn reason why," Marcus snapped. "Rex has to be the first one who gets a taste of her. He always get to sample the merchandise first. Don't worry you know he always let you have a turn."

Daria kept her body still in the chair as Marcus and Gary argued at her side. She couldn't see a thing through the blindfold covering her eyes. How in the hell was she going to get out of this situation? How long had she been out? Did Lindow and Ace know that she was missing yet?

"Look at how good her breasts look in that shirt." Gary moaned.

She didn't flinch as Gary hand's reached out and groped her breasts then moved between her legs to cop a feel. "I bet her body is so hot that it would burn your cock alive."

"You better stop touching her or Rex will kill you when he gets back." Marcus warned Gary.

"All right," Gary groaned as he removed his hand from her body. "But I still want my turn with her ass. Speaking of ass, I think that's the first place I'm going to take her."

She tried to keep her body relaxed as Gary's hand came back and touched breasts and stomach. "Do you want a shot with her too?"

"I'm not into raping a woman," Marcus sneered from behind her. "I just want to find Ronnie and get that damn money back he owes Rex. When all of this is over, I want out from under his thumb. I know he was the one who had my little sister attacked at college."

Gray once again dropped his hand from her body and from the sounds of his footsteps moved away from her. "Don't go there with Rex. If he did that shit to Ja'coby, his own nephew, you know he wouldn't have a problem killing you."

Daria was proud of herself for not gasping at that bit of information. She knew for sure now that Rex was the person after Ronnie. God, she had to get out of her and tell Lindow the truth-that she knew where Ronnie was.

"I don't care," Marcus hissed.

"Don't care about what?" She heard a third voice question as another man entered the room.

"Nothing," Marcus muttered.

"What do we have here?" the man asked. She could feel his breath on the back of her neck.

"Rex, I found Ms. Jacobs like you wanted," Gary answered. "Did I do a good job?"

"Gary, you did just as I asked and for that you will be rewarded later on," Rex answered as his fingers brushed against the side of her neck. "But first I need some time alone with the beautiful Ms. Jacobs here."

"Can I have her when you're finished?" Gary begged. "I want some of her so bad," he moaned.

"You just have to be patient and wait until I'm done with her. If there's anything left then you're welcome to it," Rex answered tugging her shirt from her pants. "Now Marcus take Gary out of here," he snapped.

"Yes sir," Marcus uttered then a few seconds later she heard the door slam shut behind her.

Grabbing her by the chin Rex ripped off the blindfold and made her look at him. "I'm not dumb as the other two. I knew you were awake the second I entered the room." He brought his face down until they were eye to eye. "I'm not going to hurt you. But if you don't do as I say I'll let Gary chloroform you again and have all the fun he wants."

Chapter Twenty Two

"Man, you need to calm down and let us do our job. We'll find Daria. She'll be okay. Marcus and Gary aren't about to harm her. They need her alive to lure Ronnie out in the open," A.J. told him for the third time in twenty minutes, but he wasn't hearing it.

This was the first time in six years that he found a woman that he wanted to spend his free time with and she was in danger because of him. He shouldn't have let her leave with Ace. Daria was under his protection and he let her down. Now, he had to find two people before either one of them got killed.

A.J. didn't know what he was talking about. What if they wanted to make an example of out of Daria? Marcus wasn't bothered in the least by shooting a woman in cold blood. For the past three years, the station had been looking into the murder of his ex-girlfriend. She was going to testify against him in another case and her body was found in the woods with two bullet holes in her head..

Marcus came up with an alibi for where he was that day, but Lindow knew that liquor store clerk had lied. It was only a matter of proving it. However, Gary terrified him more than Marcus ever would. Gary had a sickness when he came to certain women and Daria fit the profile: Young, intelligent, successful and strong-willed. The more driven a woman was, the more Gary lusted to take the power away from her and he only knew of one way. He couldn't let that happen to Daria.

"I don't care what you say. I'm going to that house. I know Rex has her." Snatching his jacket off the back of his chair, Lindow stormed towards the police entrance only to have A.J. block his path.

"Stop acting on your emotions and think like a cop for a minute. You know that if you get within ten feet of that house Rex will kill her. Right now, we both know that he wants his money back more than blood on his hands," A.J. stated trying to reason with him. "Rex is a big-time drug dealer and only murders people when he has too. Daria is safe as long as she doesn't push him too far."

"You never like her in the first place. I bet your hoping that he put a bullet in her," he accused shoved past his friend.

Grabbing him by the arm, A.J. shoved in down into the nearest chair. "Listen, the Captain is about fed up with you and your shit. He'll take you off this case without thinking twice about it. How can you save Daria if you don't have your badge and gun?

No, I'm not fond of Daria. I think she's too opinionated and a danger to herself, but I'm not the one in love with her. You are."

Lindow tossed his jacket on the floor hating the fact that A.J. was thinking more clearly than him. "I hate it when you're right."

"I'm usually the level headed one when it comes to things like this," A.J. gloated sitting on the edge of the desk. "I think the best way for us to deal with this is to see does Rex contact us."

"Do you think that he will?" Lindow questioned. "We don't have anything that he needs. He's holding all of the cards."

"Then I guess we have to get something that he is willing to trade Daria for, won't we?"

"Ronnie isn't an option," he pointed out, hating that Daria's cousin got her into this damn mess in the first place. "Neither one of us has a clue where he's at. I know half the police station has searched all over the city for him, but that little weasel is in deep hiding."

"I give the kid credit. He's good at keeping a low profile, but I know when the word gets out of the street that Rex and his boys have his cousin. He'll make contact with someone and I think you'll be the man he searches out."

Hell will freeze over before Ronnie Wells will come looking for him. "I'm not a patient man and I'm not going to sit around waiting to see what Rex has in mind for Daria." Picking his jacket up off the floor, Lindow went for the door and this time A.J. didn't try to stop him.

"I was really hoping that we could become friends. I admire your drive. I don't say that about most women I come across," Rex praised untying her legs from the chair and then her hands. "You haven't begged for me not to kill you once."

Daria rubbed her wrists trying to get the blood back into them. Rex scared the hell out of her with his cool demeanor, but he wouldn't ever find that out from her.

"I'm not going to beg for my life because you aren't planning on killing me."

"Why are you so sure?" Rex asked yanking her up from the chair. "I could already have a ditch waiting with your name on it."

Daria kept her body from flinching at Rex's threat. He wasn't serious about killing her. At least not yet, she still had something he needed. "We both know that I'm the only person Ronnie will come out of hiding for, and you need me to be alive. If you kill me and he does have your money you can bet you'll never see it again."

Rex's grip tightened painfully on her upper arm and Daria bit the inside of her cheek to keep from crying out.

"Are you saying that you know where my money is?"

"I said if..." she exclaimed hitting Rex on the arm so he would release her. "Now let go of me."

"Bitch, I'm not the kind of man you want to jerk around. It's best you remember that," he threatened before he flung her away from him.

"Do you think I like getting kidnapped from a gas station?" Daria screamed while she tried to think of a way to escape Rex. The only means of getting away she spotted was a window behind Rex. Now all she had to do was find a way to get to it.

"How does Detective Woods tolerate that mouth of yours? I would have shut it up a long time ago."

She would give anything if Lindow could be here now to help her, but he wasn't so she just had to do it herself. "Detective Woods isn't dumb enough to try it and I get the feeling you aren't either," Daria taunted stepping back.

"I'm holding back from hurting you, but keep running that mouth of yours and I will," Rex promised.

Daria was pissed Rex wasn't moving more away from the window. She couldn't quite tell how high they were up, but it didn't matter. She would jump from the eighth floor if she had to get away from him. Anything was better than being trapped like this.

"You must not value your life as much as I thought you do because you wouldn't say things like that to me," Rex threatened stalking towards her.

Great...you've done it now. You opened your mouth one too many times. He's going to get you now. Daria prepared herself for a battle and hoped she came out on the winning end.

The door flung opened behind them distracting Rex's attention from her as Marcus came rushing through.

"Boss...that detective is outside demanding to talk to you."

"Shit...does he know that she's here?" Rex questioned looking over at her.

"I don't know, but I tried to get him to leave and he isn't moving," Marcus answered glancing back out the door. "He said that he wasn't leaving until he talked to you."

"Fuck!" Rex cursed. "Detective Woods is becoming a thorn in my side. I'm getting tired of him and little Nancy Drew here in my business, but I've to deal with him first."

Heading for the door, Rex stopped at the entrance and looked back at Daria. "Don't go anywhere."

"Do you want me to stay with her?" Marcus asked.

Rex gave his head a small shake. "I need you to come with me to make sure he leaves Ms. Jacobs isn't going anywhere because she doesn't want her boyfriend killed." Rex hurried out the door followed by Marcus and it wasn't a second later when she heard the key locking her inside.

Daria didn't waste a second before she raced over to the window and tried the lock. She let out the breath she was holding when it raised with ease. Pushing it open, she slipped through it and crawled out of the roof.

Slowly making it to the edge she noticed the only way for her to get off the side was the huge oak tree in front of her. Her heart was pounding hard in her chest as she reached for a limb and swung her leg over. She hadn't climbed down a tree this size since she was eleven, playing with her brothers.

"Please God...don't let me fall and break my neck," Daria prayed as she worked her way down the tree until she was low enough to jump down. As much as she wanted to go for Woods' car it was at the front of the house and she was at the back. She wasn't going to chance Rex and his thugs trying to hurt Woods because of her.

Instead as soon as her feet hit the ground she took off across the grass towards the opposite end of the sidewalk away from Rex's house. She noticed a police car in the distance and without a doubt she knew they would help her.

Chapter Twenty Three

"Where in the hell is she? You better not have harmed her," Lindow threatened. He broke so many laws getting over here to Rex's house, but all he could think about was Daria being held her against her will.

"I'm sorry Detective Woods, but I don't know who you're referring to," Rex smirked. "Are you sure that you at the right place?"

Lindow hated how Rex thought he owned the streets and everyone who walked them, but he was going to be the man who brought him down. "Stop lying. You know I'm taking about Daria Jacobs. You're the only one who had a reason to snatch her from the gas station."

"Detective, I never took anyone from the gas station."

"Fine...then you had Marcus or Gary grab her and then bring her back here. I want you to give her to me."

"I'm not responsible for what Marcus or Gary might do when they aren't around me. Furthermore, I can't give someone back that I don't have, now can I?" Rex taunted. "So, I think it's best that you leave, detective."

"I'm not going anywhere until I search every inch of this house," Lindow brushed past Rex and headed for another room when Marcus stepped in his path."

"I think my boss told you to leave," Marcus piped up. "Besides, you can't come in here without a search warrant. How do you know that Daria didn't get tired of you and left? Come on, you do this you have what it takes to satisfy a black woman?"

Lindow's temper flared as he lunged for Marcus until someone pulled him back, "Don't do it," A.J. hissed in his ear. "You don't want to lose your badge for a punk like this."

Jerking his arms away, he shoved his partner away from him. "They have Daria and we both know it. I'm not about to leave without her. If beating the hell out of him costs me my badge then I'll do it, but I'm not waiting for a search warrant."

"Daria, isn't here," A.J. informed him.

"You're lying to me. You hate her and we both know it." Lindow snapped as he jerked his arm away.

"I'm not lying to you. Officer Davidson was patrolling this street about ten minutes ago and saw Daria running down the sidewalk. He pulled over, and got her into the police car. She's safe."

"Where is she?" Lindow asked wanting to see for himself that Daria was safe.

"I think it's safer if I don't tell you here," A.J. looking past him at Marcus and then Rex. "Let's go and I'll take you to her."

"See Detective Woods? You barge into my home and accuse me of taking your woman when actually she was just out for a little walk. Maybe you should keep her closer to you and next time she might not get lost," Rex snickered and then left the room.

"Why don't the two of you get your asses out of here? Mr. Staples is a very busy man and he doesn't waste his time on people like you," Marcus stuck out his chest like a big man, gesturing to the open door with his hand.

Lindow went towards the door and then stopped half-way there. "Marcus, I would suggest that you break your ties with Rex before he gets you sent to prison or you're found dead in an alley."

"That's enough...we've to go," A.J. said, grabbing his arm leading him out the door and down the steps to their cars.

"What in the hell is wrong with you?" A.J. shouted once they were outside. "You can't go and do shit like that. Would you have really hit Marcus if I hadn't rushed in when I did?"

"Nothing happened because you came in time, so let's forget about it. I want to know where Daria is," Lindow demanded. He was fed up with getting the run around from everyone around him.

"Officer Davidson took her back to your house and he'll stay with her until you get back there."

"He won't be there much longer," Lindow stated as he got into his car and drove off leaving A.J. standing there watching at him fade into the distance.

Lindow couldn't wait until he got home and saw that Daria was safe for himself and then he was going to shake some sense into her cute little ass. How was he supposed to focus on finding her cousin when she couldn't stay out of trouble?

After Rex and his crew had enough nerve to kidnap Daria from a gas station, he found out what she knew the whereabouts Ronnie. He wasn't about to leave her alone again. If he wasn't able to be with, her he'd make sure she had a police officer protecting her until he could.

Daria had captured a piece of his heart he thought had died a long time ago. She was slowly becoming his life and if anything else happened to her...he shivered just thinking about it. He was about two blocks from his house when he noticed the road crew putting up a detour sign because of street construction on the route he usually took home.

"I can't believe this," Lindow complained as smacked his hands against the steering wheel. "Now, I have to go up another two blocks to get back on the street I need." Lindow pulled off that street and continue to the other one that he didn't want to take.

The new street he had to take wasn't the best street in town, but he drove down it anyway. He never knew what he might see going on and if he saw something shady it was his duty as a police officer to stop and check it out. Lindow was halfway down the street when a guy came out of nowhere and ran across the street a few feet in front of him then ducked into an abandoned building across the street.

"Ronnie!" He screamed and quickly pulled over to the side of the street. Lindow got out of his car, pushed the button on his keys to lock it and ran after Ronnie. He paused by the door and looked around, but he didn't notice anything as pushed open the door, pulled out his gun and slipped inside.

There was only a minimal of light coming through the boarded up windows making it hard for his to see, but it was enough for him to notice a few empty boxes and not much else. He should have called for backup and waited for them to come, but he couldn't waste the time. Ronnie could have another way out of here and then he might not be able to find him again.

"Ronnie Wells, I'm Detective Lindow Woods and you need to come out with your hands up," he demanded from his place from behind one of the crates. "I'm not going to hurt you, but you need to turn yourself in."

Silence.

"Ronnie...I saw you run in here. There's no need for you to hide from me, I want to help you."

"Why would you want to help me?" A young voice yelled out from the semi-darkness. "You don't know a damn thing about me!"

"I know that Daria loves you and wants to help you get out of this mess," he yelled back trying to figure out where Ronnie was hiding.

"Don't you dare bring my cousin into this! She's a wonderful person and I don't want her hurt."

"I want the same thing as you do. Daria means a lot to me and I'm trying my best to keep her safe, but Rex doesn't see it the same way as we do."

"What are you talking about?" Ronnie yelled. "Has Rex done something to Daria? Is she okay?"

"I'm not going to continue to have this conversation like this. Either you show me your face or I'm out of here," Lindow lied. He wasn't about to leave this building without Ronnie.

He heard a scarping sound and a few minutes later Ronnie step from around a stack of boxes about twenty feet in front of him.

"Good...now toss any weapons you might have on the ground and kick it over her to me," Lindow ordered moving out into the open so Ronnie could see him.

Reaching back his back Ronnie pulled out a small hand gun and tossed it on the floor and then kicked it towards him. "Is Daria okay? Did Rex, Marcus or Gary hurt her?"

"No, Daria managed to escape and she's back at my house waiting for me," Lindow answered still holding his weapon on Ronnie. "I need for you to come down to the station and make a statement."

"No...the second I step into that place I'll get tossed in jail," Ronnie said taking a step back. "I'm not getting locked up again. I can't handle it."

"I'm going to place my gun back in my holster, but you can't make any sudden movements or I'll be forced to shot you." Holding up one hand, Lindow slid his gun back into his holster with the other one.

"You aren't under arrest, but you need to give a statement down at the station about Rex and the kid that died. You have to know something about it. Rex has to be after you for something besides the money."

"I can't talk he'll kill me," Ronnie shouted. "I don't want to die."

"You won't die, but you have to trust me," Lindow assured him.

Ronnie came towards him and then quickly stepped back. "I don't believe you. You're just saying that because you want to get me at that police station. I got myself into this mess and I'm going to get myself out.I'll come back to you only after I've information that clears my name. I'm not a theif. I didn't steal Rex's money and he won't leave me alone until I prove it." Spinning around he darted back into the darkness and a split second the sound of a door opening and closing echoed inside the empty warehouse.

"Son of a bitch," Lindow cursed as he pulled out his gun and raced after Ronnie, but by the time he got outside Ronnie was nowhere in sight. "Shit! What am I going to tell Daria?"

Chapter Twenty Four

He didn't know how long he stood outside the door with the keys swinging in his hands, but he just wasn't ready to go in yet. How was he going to tell Daria that he might have sent her cousin into a situation that he might not be able to get out of? Ronnie was irate when he ran out of that warehouse.

"You can do this," he said giving himself some encouragement as he unlocked the front door and went inside. Lindow heard laughter coming from the kitchen and headed in that direction.

Pausing in the doorway, he watched Daria interacting with Ace and felt a sting of jealousy that she felt so comfortable around his brother.

"Where's Officer Davidson?" he asked, tossing his keys down on the table. "I thought I told him to stay here with Daria."

"He's wife went into labor and he had to leave, so I called Ace over to stay with me," Daria replied wiping her hands on a towel. She tossed it on the table and ran over and hugged him. "I'm so glad to see you. I never thought I would get to see you again."

Lindow removed Daria's arms from around his waist and stepped back from her. "Really, you aren't acting like a woman that was held against her will by a drug dealer and his buddies. I thought you would be in tears not baking cookies with my brother having a good old time," he snapped angry more at himself than Daria.

"Maybe A.J. is right and you're in this with them. Do you know where the money is and all of this has been an act to sucker me in? Answer me! Are you the lying con-artist that my partner believes that you are?"

"You son of a bitch," Daria hissed. "I don't have to take this shit from you. I'm outta here," she snapped brushing past him running out of the room.

"What in the hell is wrong with you?" Ace growled rushing up to him. "Do you know how long it took me to get her to come out of that bedroom? God... Officer Davidson left me a note to keep an eye on her because he was concerned about her. He had called one of the female officers over here to talk to her, but she wouldn't do it."

"Why did she come out of the room for you? What makes my little brother so damn special?" Lindow hated that Ace was able to touch a part of Daria that he wasn't.

"You're such an idiot. Daria didn't come out of that room for me, she came out for you."

"I'm not following you."

"I told Daria that you wouldn't want her in there hiding away like Rex had the power over her. You would want her out here being strong until you came home and then she could talk to you about what happened. It wasn't even her idea to make the cookies. It was mine. I had to make the time pass for her somehow."

Lindow's heart fell to the pit of his stomach. He felt like he was something that belonged on the bottom of someone's shoe. How could he say those things to Daria after what she had been through today?

"Ace, shit, I've really stuck in foot in it this time," he mumbled running his fingers through his hair.

Ace grabbed his jacket off the back of the chair and patted him on the back. "I wouldn't want to be you," he sighed then left the room closing the back door behind him.

He didn't know how long he stayed inside the kitchen thinking of a way to apologize to Daria. Why did this one woman bring out so many emotions inside of him? All Daria had to do was smile at him and she had him wrapped around her little finger.

"I might as well get it over with," he gathered his courage, leaving the kitchen and heading for Daria's room. Lindow knocked once but he didn't get an answer.

"*Inamorata*, please open the door. I want to talk to you." He knocked again trying to coach Daria out into the hallway.

"Leave me alone. I don't want to talk to you right now," she yelled through the door.

"Please sweetheart, let me in. I can't apologize properly through this stupid door."

"Just go away. I'm tired and the only thing I want to do is go to bed."

"Daria, we aren't going to bed mad at each other. You've been through a horrible experience today and you need to talk about it. You let my brother in. Why won't you let me?"

The door flung open with such force that it banged against the wall. "Ace doesn't toss accusations in my face every time we get with ten feet of each other. He listens to me instead of ordering me around all the time. Your brother is the kind of man every woman dreams of falling in love with." Daria threw at him before trying to slam the door back in face.

"He can't have you," Lindow snarled holding the door with his hand. "Ace isn't the man for you. He's too young and you'll get tired of him after a week. You need a man that's going to challenge that stubborn streak that races through your veins."

Giving the door a slight push, Lindow came into the bedroom forcing Daria to take a step back and the slammed the door shut behind him. "I really don't want you getting any ideas about my brother. "

"Why not?" she questioned, folding her arms over her chest. "Ace is an amazing man and I enjoy being around him. We already have something in common."

"What in the fuck to you have in common with Ace?"

"I don't have to tell you anything. It's none of your business," Daria replied in a harsh tone.

"That's where you're wrong," Lindow responded, in a low, husky tone grabbing her by the arm tugging her closer to him. "Everything that goes on with you is my business." He bent his head and ran his tongue along side of Daria's neck. "Hmmm...you take like strawberries."

"Stop trying to seduce me," she moaned shoving at his chest. "I'm mad at you."

"Let me make it up to you. I'm very good at apologizing." Nibbling his way up her neck, Lindow tried to control his need as his cock grew painful hard in his jeans. It had been so long since he had been wrapped in Daria's wet heat.

"Lindow, please I'm not ready."

Moving his head, his eyes traveled over her face and searched her eyes. Lindow saw some of the trust he had gain still lurking there, it might disappear if he handled this situation badly. He wasn't ready to lose the part of Daria that took him so long to gain.

Linking their fingers together, he led her over to the bed. "Go ahead and lay down. I'll stay with you until you fall asleep." He had to show Daria that there was a soft side to him if he was ever going to gain her love.

"You're alright with this? You won't handcuff me to the bed or anything?"

"Not unless it you want it," he winked.

"Lin..."

"Daria, get into the bed and get some rest. We have a lot to talk about in the morning," Lindow sighed ushering her under the covers. Lying on top he wrapped his arm around her waist.

"Aren't you going to get under the covers too?" Daria glanced over her shoulder pinning him with those eyes he loved so much.

"Not unless you want to something else besides sleep," he whispered by her ear.

"Good night, Lindow." She murmured turning away snuggling deep under the covers.

"Sleep tight, *il mio amore*."

He didn't know how long he had been out before the sound of his cell phone ringing woke him up. Taking a peek at Daria, Lindow rolled off the bed and answered it.

"Yeah...what is it?'

"We found a body in the alley," A.J. informed him.

"Don't tell me that it's Ronnie." Lindow eased out of the bedroom and closed the door behind him. He couldn't handle if he got Daria's cousin murder. She wouldn't ever be able to forgive him.

"I don't want to get into this over the phone. You just need to come down to the alley where Marcus and Gary had Daria trapped. Whatever you do don't bring her with you."

"What not?" Lindow questioned wondering what in the hell was wrong on. "What's going on in the alley where they had Daria?"

"Listen to me just don't bring her and get down here," A.J. demanded ending the phone call. "An officer is already on his way to your house to stay with Daria. This isn't good at all."

Coming back into the room, he made sure that Daria was okay and then quickly left so he wouldn't wake her up. "I pray that A.J. is wrong and it isn't Ronnie because Daria isn't going to be able to handle it."

Covering his mouth with a cloth Lindow raced from the alley while trying to keep nausea from coming up. Who in the hell butchered Ronnie's body like that? How could some cut him up like that and leave him in that trash barrel? Removing the cloth, he shoved it back in his pocket and took several deep breaths trying to calm down his nerves.

"I told you it was bad," A.J. said coming up behind him. "I almost lost my lunch when I saw all the blood by the dumpster. I only thought shit like that happen in the movies. I never took Rex for the type to cause that kind of torture on a person."

"I can't tell Daria about this. She'll be devastated." He was numb with increasing rage and shock. "I know that bastard Rex had a hand in this. I told Ronnie not to confront him about the drugs, but he won't listen."

"You spoke with Ronnie today?" A.J. asked, coming around to stand in front of him, "When did this happen?"

Torment was eating him from the inside and there was nothing that he could do about it. "It doesn't matter now. Ronnie is dead and Daria isn't going to forgive me for allowing it to happen. How do I tell you that her family can't even see the body?"

"Man...I'm not the one to ask. In my ten year career I have never been involved in a case like this before." A.J. sighed patting him on the shoulder. "We should go back in there to make sure everything is by the book."

"Damn it to hell. I hate this. It wasn't supposed to turn out like this. Why didn't Ronnie listen to me?" Lindow wondered out loud as he followed A.J. back into the gruesome scene.

Moving out of the shadows the figure slipped past the two police officers while they ushered a group of people away from the table. She pressed her body against the wall trying to keep out of the lights, but she had to find out what was going on. Lindow had snuck out of the house like a theif in the night and she knew it involved her cousin. It was hard for her to get dressed in record time after eavesdropping on his conversation.

Daria got close as she could and noticed all the blood on the ground around a trashcan. She stood still next to the building as two officers from earlier walked paused by her hiding place.

"I can't believe how someone cut up his body," said officer closer to her.

"It looked like something out of a horror movie. Each part of his body was cut up and tossed in there. I heard there was even a note tapped to his shirt." The second officer stated. "I know that Detective Woods had been looking for the Wells' boy of a while, but I know he didn't want to find his body inside a trashcan."

Daria couldn't keep the screams busting from her throat as she rushed past the officers towards the scene. "Oh my God, Ronnie!!"

Two strong arms picked her up and carried her from the alley as she struggled inside the tight grip, "Put me down! I've to see my cousin. It isn't him. I know it isn't him," she screamed scratching at the arm that wouldn't release her. It's a lie! I know it is."

"Daria, calm down or you'll coming to make yourself sick," Lindow whispered in her ear carrying her away from the scene. "How did you even know I was here?"

"Let go of me. I've to see that body. I know it isn't my cousin," she cried hitting at his arms.

"No...baby it's not something you want to see. That shouldn't be the last imagine you have of Ronnie. It's him. I saw his face. It's him."

As the reality of what Lindow was telling her, Daria tore herself away with a choking cry and fell down the ground. "I failed. I wasn't able to save him," she wept loudly, rocking back and forth. "I got my cousin murdered. I should have told you I knew where he was. I kept lying to you and it got Ronnie killed. I'm to blame for this. It's all my fault."

"Stop saying that. It wasn't your fault that Ronnie got murdered. Whoever was after him finally caught up with him," Lindow started falling down beside her. He didn't have to heart to tell her that he already knew about her meeting with Ronnie. If he came clean about that, then he would have to confess he saw Ronnie earlier today. Daria wouldn't be able to handle it not with everything going on right now. He would tell her later when the time was better, but he couldn't wait too long. He had to find out what Ronnie might have told her.

He tried to touch her again, but she pushed him away. "Don't touch me! While I was at your house in bed Ronnie was getting dismembered."

"I swear to you baby. That I'll find out who did this and put them deep under the jail. They won't get away with this."

She closed her eyes, her heart aching with pain. Daria brushed away her remaining tears with the back of her hands as the poured down her face. "I can't get into this with you. I need to make arrangements for Ronnie's burial." Opening her eyes, she stood up and fixed her clothes. "I've to go back home."

A suffocating sensation tightened in Lindow's throat was he watched Daria distance herself away from him. "Don't shut me out. Let me help you get through this. Sweetheart, I'm in love with you."

Her eyes widened in alarm as Daria stumbled back from him, "I can't deal with this. Not now. This isn't the time or the place for this, Woods."

"Fuck...stop calling me that everything you get scared or hurt!" Lindow screamed fed up with the way Daria controlled her emotions when it came to him. "I'm in love with you and I've been for a very long time."

"Don't you understand this isn't about whether or not I'm in love with you right now? I've to take care of my family. They are the most important thing in my life. I promised them that I would bring Ronnie back home safe and I didn't. I'm no better than the people who murdered him."

"Stop...please don't" Daria begged holding up her hands as he tried to comfort her. "I can't handle you touching me. I need all of my composure to get through the phone calls and dealing with my parents once I get back home."

Lindow felt helpless at the sound of the defeat in Daria's voice. He had to tell her the truth. It wasn't her fault that Ronnie got killed. It was his. "Let me go with you. I can take some time off."

"No. You need to stay here and find out who killed him. I'll call you after everything gets settled at home."

"Why don't I believe you?" he questioned.

"Please just let me leave and I'll be back."

"Go," Lindow relented, "but remember that I love you and I'm not giving up on us."

A flicker of apprehension coursed through Daria at the thought of having to deal with Ronnie's murder and her growing feelings for Lindow at the same time. She wasn't going to be able to manage both. One of them who have to be placed on the back burner and unfortunately it was going to be Lindow.

"I'm just staying long enough to get Ronnie's body signed over to me and then I'm going back home."

"I understand. Let me find someone to take you back home and stay with you until I come back."

"There's no need for that," she stated.

"It's my job to keep you safe and I'm going to do that until you get on that plane," Lindow exclaimed brushing his knuckles down the side of her face.

"Thank you," she whispered.

"Don't thank me. I love you and I'm going to keep you safe." Dropping his hand, Lindow linked their fingers together and took her over to a police car.

Chapter Twenty Five

A cool breeze danced across her skin as she watched Ronnie's coffin as it was lowered into the ground. The past two weeks almost broke her but she held up for her family. Lindow had been calling her, but she couldn't talk to him now. Not since she was about to get her hands on a copy of the note tape to Ronnie's shirt. Why didn't he tell her he had talked to her cousin hours before he was murdered? What happened between the two of them? Where had Ronnie gone that caused his death?

Holding her face up to the sun she allowed the heat to dry the tears off her cheeks. God, she could still hear her mother's scream after she finally told them about the condition of Ronnie's body. Neither of her parents had wanted to spread his ashes, so they went the extra expense and had the urn buried inside a coffin. They wanted a place to come to visit him.

"Daria, who is that man standing of there by those trees?" her father asked as the preacher finished the prayer. "He has been standing there since the funeral started."

Following the lines of trees she instantly recognized the build and her heart skipped a beat, "I know who it is. Why don't you take mama back home and I can deal with this?" She responded heading for their unwanted guest.

It only took her a matter of minutes before she stopped in front of the man who has been tormenting her dreams since the second she met him. "Why are you here? I thought I told you over the phone that you wouldn't be welcomed."

"I came to pay my respects and see you. I want to explain about the note," he answered.

"We have nothing to say to each other. I don't know what you said to Ronnie, but whatever it was got him killed. I can't look at you and not think about that."

"Whoever planted that note is lying and when I find out who I'll know who murdered you cousin."

Daria was tired of fighting the battle. It wasn't worth it anymore. Ronnie was dead so what was the use of dealing with anything else. She needed to part ways with Lindow and move on with her life. They wouldn't ever be able to get over this to have a healthy loving relationship.

"Please just leave me and my family alone. I can't handle anymore of this. I only want to be able to mourn my cousin and then move on with my life. I suggest that you do the same thing." Daria gave Lindow last long look and then headed away from him.

"I'm not giving up on us. I'm going to solve this murder and get you back, do you hear me," Lindow yelled after her, but she kept going wishing with all her heart that she still wasn't in love with the man behind her.

Sitting inside his car, Lindow glanced at his watch for the third time in the span of ten minutes. Ever since he came home last month from visiting Daria all of his time and focus had been on finding out who murdered Ronnie and where the lost money was.

The passenger side door and his informant slid closed the door. "I didn't think you were going to show up."

"I'm here, but I'm not saying that I trust you one bit. How can I after all the things you did to Daria? How do I know this isn't a plan to hurt me? We haven't been on the best of terms. I was the one who arrested you a few years ago for selling stolen guns."

"Man…I know all of that, but I can't keep quiet about this. If I don't turn on Rex after what he did, I know he'll find a way to make it seem like I was involved." The person next to him squirmed around in the seat. "He scares the hell out of me now. I don't want to be a part of his crew anymore."

"It has to be something more than that. Rex made you a part of his group right out of high school. Now you just want to up and leave it. It doesn't make any sense," Lindow exclaimed, taking a glance at the individual next to him. "Either tell me the truth or the deal is off and I'll find someone else to help take down Rex."

"Alright, shit I'll tell you. Rex knew all along who attacked my sister and never said a word. I only find out when I overheard him talking to Gary," Marcus growled. "Now, I know I don't have the best record in town and you think I murdered my ex-girlfriend, but I didn't. Gary did that, but I don't have any proof."

Lindow wanted to take Marcus at his word, but it was hard to after the life of crime the man next to him had led over the last seven years. "What do you want to get out of this? I can't guarantee you won't get any jail time for kidnapping Daria."

"I'm not worried about that. All I want is to make Rex and Gary pay for that shit they did to my sister and Ronnie."

"Are you saying that Ronnie never stole that money from Rex?" Lindow questioned.

"No, he never had the money but Rex didn't know that. He was fed a lot of lies by Gary and he ate them up."

"Why would Rex believe a low-life like Gary?"

"I really don't have an answer for that, but Gary took that money and gave it to someone for safekeeping." Marcus continued, but it seemed like he was holding something back.

"I think you know who he gave that money to. You and Gary are close, he had to confide in you about it," he insisted, wanting any kind of information that he could take back to Daria. He had so much to prove to her now.

"Listen, I'm not getting involved that deep. I told you what I know. I hope you use it as best as you can." Marcus pulled the hood on his jacket over his head. "I can't let anyone find out I talked to you or I'll end up like Ronnie."

"Tell me what you know and I can put you and your family under witness protection."

Snickering Marcus opened the door, "Are you referring to that messed up witness protection that wasn't able to keep that lawyer chick hid from Gary. I'll think I'll pass," he blew off the suggestion and got out of the car slamming the door behind him.

Starting up the car Lindow pulled out of the alley and drove back towards his house, but he couldn't get Marcus' comment out of his head. Why didn't he want the police station to protect him? Did he know who told Gary where Daria was staying that first night she arrived? He was going to get down to the bottom of this case because his life was on the line.

Chapter Twenty Six

Sitting outside in the car, she stared at the house and wondered for the hundredth time what in the hell she was doing? Why didn't she just stay in Washington, D.C. and forget all about him? He was trouble with a capital T, but she couldn't stop thinking about him.

These last few weeks had been the hardest of her life. She'd never understand how someone so arrogant found his way into her heart, but that's what Lindow Woods had done and she was having a hell of a time getting him out.

Daria debated if she should just drive off and take the next plane back home without even letting him know that she was here. He would only try to find a way into talking her into staying with him and only bad stuff could happen from that.

Like her falling in love with him when she wasn't looking for a man in her life. It was so funny how life turned out. Her one vow to herself was never to date a man she had to deal with on a personal level and now here she was sitting out Lindow's house.

"I guess it's now or never." Opening the door Daria got out and made her way towards the front door. Raising her hand she knocked once and then waited for an answer, but none came. "I know he's home his car is in the driveway." She turned the door handle and it swung open.

Stepping inside the house, she called out. "Lindow, are you here? It's me Daria. We need to talk." She went further inside and shut the door behind her. "Lindow, are you here?" she yelled again, but still didn't get a response.

Wondering what was going on Daria slowly eased her way down the hallway to Lindow's bedroom. A bad feeling settled in the pit of her stomach and she pushed open the door. She felt for the light on the side of the wall and flicked it on with her hand and then screamed at the sight of Lindow lying unconscious on the floor in a pool of blood.

"Lindow!" His name was wrenched from her throat as she raced over to him. Thinking quickly she felt for a pulse and let out a sigh of relief when she found one.

"At least he isn't dead. Baby, don't worry. I'm going to call an ambulance." She pushed her body up from the floor and raced over to the phone.

"I won't do that if I were you," a voice advised behind her.

Spinning around she took a quick step back stumbling into the table behind her. "What are you doing here? I'm not scared of you. I'll kill you if I've to," Daria promised watching Gary as he waved the gun at her.

"You'll do no such thing if you don't want lover boy more hurt than he already is," Gary threatened swinging the gun from her back over to Lindow. "I don't mind killing a cop."

"What do you want?" God, she wished that she had some kind of weapon to use against him. He wasn't going to get a free shot at her. "I'm not going anywhere with you."

"Then I guess you don't want to find out who killed your precious cousin," he snickered taunting her.

"You bastard tell me who killed him. It was you wasn't it and your sick friend Marcus, wasn't it? The two of you got tired of waiting for your money and you butchered him then tossed him in that alley."

"Slut...I didn't touch a hair on your cousin's head. I did dispose of the body, but I wasn't the one who cut him up. I'm not a sick fuck like that. Plus, Marcus wasn't even around when it happened, but I told him all about it afterwards. If I was going down so was he."

"Tell me who did it," Daria screamed as her heart pounded so hard inside of her chest she felt like it was going to burst.

"Come with me and you'll find out everything."

"I don't trust you."

"You shouldn't trust me, but this doesn't have anything to do with me wanting you. It's all about business now, baby and someone is waiting to see you. Now are you coming or not?" Gary demanded.

"What about Detective Woods? We can't leave him here like that. He's needs a doctor. Let me call an ambulance for him," she begged trying to stall for time.

"Head wounds always look worse than they are. I didn't hit him that hard, so he could be awake pretty soon. It will give us enough time to get where we are going."

Grabbing her by the arm, Gary yanked her from the room and placed the gun against her head when she tried to struggle. "Please give me a reason to shoot you," he begged. "It would give me such pleasure to get rid of you."

Daria quit fighting Gary and let him drag her from the house. Going to the back of a car parked across the street, he popped open the trunk and shoved her inside. She didn't know how long Gary drove until the car finally stopped and she was yanked from the trunk by one arm.

Taking her across the street, he shoved her around the side of a building and forced her to stop in front of a ladder that led up to the roof. "Don't stand there like an idiot. Climb that damn thing and don't try to anything funny. You'll be dead before the thought leaves your mind."

The pain in his head was like nothing that he has ever felt before sitting up, Lindow pressed two fingers to the back of his head and they came away bloody. "What hit me?" he groaned as he got up off the floor. It took him a few minutes to get his surrounding and then he inched his way to the kitchen.

Opening the freezer, he grabbed an ice pack and placed it on the back of his head. Lindow thought back to what happened, but it was still a little fuzzy. He recalled walking into his bedroom, turning on the light and then moving towards the bed followed by a sharp pain in his head.

"Who in the world hit me and why were they in my house?" He couldn't understand why all of this was happening to him. It was like his life was going down his since Daria forbid him to have any contact with her. He hadn't been able to sleep at all. He removed the ice pack from his head and flung it into the sink.

"I've to get over my feelings for Daria. She doesn't want me and I don't blame her," Lindow exclaimed as he headed out of the kitchen. The sound of his cell phone ringing made him stop in the hallway.

"Woods," he answered.

"Lindow, I need you down at the old warehouse off 5th street," A.J. said. "I've Gary cornered on the inside, but I need help."

"How long have you been there?" he questioned going straight for the door shaking off his dizzy headache as the best he could.

"About an hour but I haven't gone on the inside yet, I see some movement on the roof I think he has made his way up there. After I get off the phone with you I'm headed that away."

"Don't go there without back up," he hollered as he ran out the door. "I'm on my way."

"Hurry up before he makes a run for it. This might be our only chance to catch him alone." The phone went dead as A.J. ended the phone call on his end.

"God. I hope nothing happens to A.J. He knows better to chase after Gary without backup," Lindow complained as he got into his car and sped off.

Easing out of his car Lindow pulled out his gun glancing around the area, he looked for a sign of A.J., but he didn't see any at all. He told his partner to stay put and he didn't. Now he only hoped that A.J. wasn't lying bleeding somewhere or worst dead. Lindow's steps pondered as he wondered should he go on or wait for the backup he called from the car.

"A.J. are you hurt?" He called out in a low voice.

"A.J. isn't here, but I am," another voice answered stepping out from the darkness.

Rising his gun higher, Lindow spun to his left at the same time Gary came out from behind the dumpster with a gun in his hand. "Hello, detective it has been a long time since I saw you. How's that sexy lady lawyer friend of yours?"

"Shut up about Daria and tell me where my partner is, you little creep."

Gary made a clucking sound with his tongue. "Now is that anyway to talk to the man that knows where you partner is?"

"I'm not playing with you. Tell me about A.J."

"A.J. is fine. The last time I saw your lazy ass partner, he was headed up to the roof. That dummy actually thought I was up there. Can he get any dumber?"

"You need to stop running your mouth and put your hands behind your back. You're under arrested for the attempted rape of Daria Jacobs and the murder of Ronnie Wells." Lindow waited for Gary to move, but he stayed right where he was.

"I'm not going back to jail for anyone. I'll let you kill me first," Gary threatened, pointing his gun directly at him.

"Put your weapon down and do as I said." He didn't want to have the burden of killing Gary on his conscience but if he had to he would.

"I already told you that I wasn't going back to jail," Gary hollered then fired his gun, but luckily the bullet went past Lindow giving him time to get a shot off.

Lindow didn't waste any time firing back and it landed point blank in Gary's chest and his body crumbled to the ground. With his gun still drawn, he eased over the body kicking the gun out of the way. Bending down, he pressed two fingers against the side of Gary's neck checking for a pulse, but he didn't find one.

"Why didn't you listen?" Lindow questioned as he stood back up. He always felt bad when a young life got taken because of the streets. Not wasting any time he sprinted over to the door that lead up to the roof and went through.

Busting through the other side, he stumbled in his tracks at the sight that met him on the other side. “A.J. what are you doing? Daria, what in the hell are you doing here? What in the fuck is going on?”

Chapter Twenty Seven

"I'm glad that you finally decided to join us," A.J. taunted jerking Daria more in front of his body as a shield. "I've been waiting here a while for you. What happened to the devil-may-care cop that I partnered up with all those years ago?"

"People change and I wanted something more in my life then the job and I recall a time that you did too. We used to sit on stakeouts fantasizing about the wives and kids we were going to have. I found my dream come true with Daria, so please don't hurt her," he begged.

"You've become such a wimp ever since you laid eyes on Little Miss Attorney. God, man you were blindsided by her and I couldn't ever make you see it. I should just kill her just to shut you the hell up." A.J. stood next to the edge of the roof and looked over. "It would be a long way down for her."

"A.J. don't do it. We can talk about this," Lindow spoke in a calm voice, so he wouldn't set his partner off. He placed his gun back into his holster and held up his hands.

"Don't use that tone of voice with me. I'm not some fucking suspect that needs to be talked down from a high. This little bitch ruined everything for me," A.J. said in a nasty tone jerking Daria by the arm.

"How did she ruin things for you?" Lindow asked, easing a step closer to A.J. in hopes of getting a chance to snatch Daria away from him.

"Everything was fine until she stuck her nose into my business. I had a good deal with Gary. We were going to split the money and then both go our separate ways. But here came this bitch trying to find her cousin and it was only a matter of time before she found out the connection between me and Gary."

"A.J., Daria doesn't know your secret about Gary. Hell, all you have to do is let her go and move back. We can talk about things. You've been under a lot of stress and have made some bad decisions."

"Listen to him," Daria chimed in for the first time since the conversation started. "I know it must been hard for you working all those long hours on a case you hated. Stress can happen to the best of us."

"Shut up," A.J hissed wrapping his arm tighter around Daria. "I didn't ask for your damn opinion. You're the reason my brother is dead. I should have let him kill you back at Lindow's instead of bringing you here to me."

"Gary was your brother," Lindow gasped clearly taken back by the news. "I never knew about this. Have you always known?"

"I found out about him about two years ago and I embraced him. I was there for him when he needed me."

A question hammered at Lindow while he watched A.J. struggled with keeping a firm hold on Daria. "Where you the one that told Gary about Daria the first night she came here?"

"You bet I was. I was helping my little brother out. He didn't deserve jail for threatening this slut," A.J. snapped with a crazed look in his eyes. "I wasn't going to let a woman beat me."

"I wasn't trying to do anything to you. I didn't know you existed until I came to Nevada. I only wanted to get my cousin out of the trouble he was in, but I failed," Daria swore moving her body around trying to break free.

Lindow noticed how Daria continued struggles were pissing off A.J. and hated that he couldn't do more for her, but one wrong move on his part would get her killed.

"Stop moving or I'm going to toss you off this building. Don't test me because I'm not playing with you," A.J. barked giving Daria a hard jerk as he pulled her closer to the edge of the building.

"Baby, please stop," Lindow begged staring at Daria. "Just be still and I'm going to get you out of this."

"That's just like you," A.J. murmured sarcastically. "You're always making promises that you can't keep."

"A.J. focus your attention on me and leave Daria out of this. Your problem is with me. I was the one who brought her here."

"You aren't ever going to let that hero complex go are you?" A.J. questioned then kissed the side of Daria's head. "Would you be willing to die for her? Is she that important to you?"

"Yes...I would die for her without thinking twice about it," Lindow said pulling his gun back out of his holster. "But no one is going to die tonight. Step back from her and raise your hands above your head. I really don't want to shoot you, but I will."

"I know you would...but the question is...are you fast enough to kill me before I toss her over the edge?" Without another warning A.J. hurled Daria over the edge with a sickening crooked smile on his face.

Seconds later Lindow fired his gun hitting A.J. in the middle chest and the impact tossed his partner over the edge as Daria's screams echoed through the air. Throwing his gun down on the ground, he raced over where Daria went over. "Please don't let her be dead," Lindow cried as his heart thumped madly as he looked over to the edge wishing for the best.

A.J.'s body was lying in a crumbled heap in a pool of blood on the cement as a crowd started to gather around the scene, but he didn't see Daria nowhere in sight.

"Lindow, please help me. I can't hold on much longer," Daria cried up to him.

Leaning more over the side, he struggled to maintain his composure at the sight of Daria holding on to a piece of roof sliding that was barely hanging on by a thread. "Baby, don't, let go. I'm going to get you."

"Please don't let me die," she begged up at him as another piece of the metal gave away.

"Do you trust me?" he asked tossing his jacket to the ground.

"Yes, I trust you."

"Good...then you have to believe that I'm going to save you. Now...I'm going to lean over the edge and when I tell you to let go. I want you to give me your left hand."

"NO! You aren't strong enough to pull me up. I'll fall just like A.J," she cried.

Lindow had no doubt that he outweighed Daria by over a hundred pounds at least. He would have no problem pulling her smaller frame back up, but she had to trust him enough to do it. He had no intention of allowing the love of his life to fall to her death.

"Daria, you've to trust me more than you've trust anyone else in your whole entire life. I love you more than any other person in my life and I swear I won't let you fall."

She swallowed hard, lifted her chin, and boldly met his gaze. "I believe you. I'm ready when you are."

He was so proud of the determination and strength that he heard in his woman's voice. After all of this was behind them he was going to treat her to a long hot bath and a massage. She deserved that and so much more.

"Sweetheart...on the count of three I want you to let go with your left hand and I'll grab it, alright?"

"Alright," the small acknowledgement came from Daria as she blinked away her tears.

"One...two...three...Now!" he screamed reaching down as Daria let go of the sliding with her left hand. Lindow quickly latched on his woman's wrist with a strong hold. "Let go and give me your right hand."

Daria gave him a little nod and then let go. Her hand wasn't in the air a minute before he wrapped his fingers around it and slowly pulled her up until she was safely back on the roof with him.

Picking her up Lindow carried Daria to the middle of the surface far away from the edge. "I can't believe I almost lost you," he cried, hugging her to his body rocking her back and forth slowly. He had felt a momentary panic as Daria's arm had left the metal and reached for his. What if he hadn't been quick enough or strong enough to pull her up?

"Lindow, you're holding me too tight," her muffled voice whispered against his shirt.

"I'm sorry," he apologized moving back. Lindow ran his hands over Daria's soft curves making sure everything was like it was supposed to be. How could she forgive him after all the things that had happened to her since he came into her life?

The sound of the roof door banging open drew his attention away from Daria to Captain Bell and several other uniformed officers racing onto the roof. "Lindow, what in the hell happened? Why are there two dead bodies down there on one of them is an officer?"

Pulling Daria up next to him, Lindow didn't know how to tell him Captain Bell about A.J. and his part in the murder of Ronnie Wells. "A.J. and Gary were brothers. They were working together along with Rex to rid of Daria and Ronnie."

"I'm not following you," Captain Bell frowned. "A.J. was a dirty cop? I don't believe you. He was a little no holds barred sometime, but he couldn't have been dirty. I would have known."

"I was his partner for years and he kept the truth about Gary from me," Lindow exclaimed. "I would have never known a thing if he hadn't confessed to me."

"Captain Bell, Detective Woods is telling the truth. A.J. was the one who told Gary where I was staying the first night I came here. His greed for the money and the power that came with it almost got me raped and murder," Daria cut in. "I'm not sorry that him or Gary are dead."

Lindow heard Daria's words and it felt like she was silently including him in that list too, but he didn't say a word. "Captain, we need to send someone to Rex's house and make sure that he doesn't get away. He's the only person left to charge with the murder of Ronnie Wells."

"Fine...I'll send someone over there now, but I'm not finished with you, Woods," Captain Bell told him before moving away.

Lindow waited until Captain Bell was out of hearing distance before he asked Daria his question. "What are you doing here?"

"I came here to see you. I want to talk to you about us," she said, looking up at him with those big brown eyes that he loved so much. "When I got to your house I knocked on the door and no one answered, so I went inside and then Gary snatched me and brought me here."

The knowledge that he almost got Daria hurt again twisted and turned at something inside of him. He couldn't let this go on. Lindow shoved his hands inside his pockets and his shoulders hunched forward as he came to an agonizing decision.

"Daria, this can't go on any longer."

"What can't go on?" She frowned.

"We can't keep going back and forth like this. It isn't good for either one of us," Lindow uttered trying to keep the pain out of his voice. "I think it's time for us to go our separate ways."

A glazed look of shock and disbelieve began to spread over her face as Daria stared at him. "No...you don't mean that. I know you care about me."

"I did care about you, but that's over now. The case has been solved and we both can move on to something new. I'll give my statement to Captain Bell and then I'll check to see what he needs from you. After that I'll see if you can get an officer to take you to the airport, maybe you'll be lucky enough to get a flight back home." Lindow tried to move away from Daria, but the soft touch of her hand on his arm stopped him.

"I do not believe a word that is coming out of your mouth, but I understand that you're still in shock about your partner. I'll let it go for now, but listen to me and listen to me good. It isn't over between us, Lindow. I love you."

He sighed heavily, his voice filled with anguish as he gently removed Daria's hand off his arm. "This is one thing that I'm not kidding about. It's over between us." Reluctantly, Lindow walked away from the love of his life, his movements stiff and awkward wondering how he was going to live the rest of his life without her.

Epilogue

The smell of the fresh sea air it him as he opened the window and pulled back the curtains inside his new home, Lindow stepped back and watched a couple walking along the beach holding hands. He tried not to give into his loneliness, but his missed the hell out of Daria.

She kept him on his toes like no other woman he had ever been with and he let all of that go, but it was for the best. He couldn't let her keep getting into dangerous situations because of him.

"I did the right thing by leaving her. She's better off without me," Lindow said out loud, trying to convince himself. "Okay...it's time that I stop hiding out here in the house. I've to get out and meet people. I'm pretty sure that Daria has already forgotten about me."

Moving away from the window, Lindow picked up his keys off the side table and went out the door slamming it shut behind him. During his run on the beach, he realized that his overgrown sense of responsibility made him give up Daria. How could he stand there and let her leave him? The independent quality that made him fall in love with her is what would have torn them apart in the end.

The madness in her life was over and Daria wouldn't need him to rescue her anymore, yet it wasn't like he did the best job of saving her from bad situations in the first place. Why was he doing this to himself, Lindow thought as his tennis shoes pounded on the sand leading him back in the direction of his house.

It was pointless to deny his love for Daria. They had all the pieces to build a wonderful relationship if he hadn't ruined it by running away from her. "I can't go on like this. I need her in my life and I'm not going to give up until I have her back."

Lindow took the steps two at a time as he hurried back to his front door and unlocked it. He rushed into his bedroom and stopped at the sight of a thick black book lying in the middle of his bed.

"I know I didn't leave that here," he murmured moving closer for a better look. "Where in the hell did it come from?" Picking it up, Lindow reads the sensual passages written on the inside.

"It's mine," a soft familiar voice confessed behind him sending his body into instant arousal.

"How did you know where I was at?" Lindow asked. Spinning around his eyes drank up the sight of Daria standing in the doorway wearing a lavender sundress looking too good for his lonely heart.

"Your Captain told me."

"Why are you here? I thought I told you we shouldn't see each other anymore." *Please let her be here because she's in love with me,* he thought.

"Do you really have to ask me that question?"

"Yes...I do, because if you're here for me to help you with another case then my answer is no."

"Lindow, I don't want you to help me work on another case," Daria answered coming further in the room. "I love you and want to spend the rest of my life with you. I missed the hell out of you and it pissed me off that you ran away from me and my love."

His body vibrated with a new found energy, Daria loved him-all was right with the world. "Baby, I love you too," Lindow murmured. "I want to spend the rest of my life with you too."

"Sorry...it's not going to be that easy for you now. You've to pay the price for leaving me for almost a month," she scolded, but he saw the twinkle in her eyes.

"Please...tell me who I can redeem myself in your gorgeous eyes," Lindow asked playing along.

Tapping the pen in her hand against her leg, Daria glanced down at the book in his hand and then back into his eyes. "You've to fill that book up with a new Daria-to-do list. I was thinking about using a blindfold or something new like that. What do you think?"

"It would be my pleasure." Lindow's deep voice rumbled as he quickly tossed the journal and pen to the side, because he didn't want to waste one second working on a sexy new addition on the Daria-to do list.

The End

To find out more about her visit her web site:

www.freewebs.com/irwriter

More about Marie Rochelle:

Marie Rochelle is a bestselling author of interracial romances featuring black women and white men. Marie first started writing IR books about two years ago and it has been nonstop for her ever since. Her first best selling IR romance was entitled Taken by Storm.

In addition, Marie has a very successful series called The Men of CCD and right now she's working on the much awaited third book in the series: Tempting Turner.

Marie has enjoyed writing from a very young age and is happy she decided to turn her career toward the IR market; a market that she had enjoyed for years herself. She has always dreamt of being a writer and now is truly happy to see her dreams becoming a reality.

Marie Rochelle books

Red Rose Publishing:

Beneath the Surface-Available Now

Pamper Me- Available Now

Be With you – Available Now

Cover Model – Available Now

With all my Heart – Available Now

Blindsided

Love Play – Coming Soon

Tycoon Club Series

Junk 'N' Trunk

Special Delivery 2: Heat Me Up- coming soon

Cobblestone Press

Special Delivery- Available Now

Phaze

All The Fixin- Available Now

My Deepest Love

Outlaw: Caught Coming May 5, 2008

A Taste of Love: Richard – Coming Soon June 30th 2008

Loving True – Coming Soon

Taken by Storm- Coming

5678420R0

Made in the USA
Lexington, KY
07 June 2010